WED TO THE ICE GIANT

Arranged Monster Mates

Layla Fae

Copyright © 2023 Layla Fae

All rights reserved

The characters and events portrayed in this book are fictitious. Any similarity to real persons, living or dead, is coincidental and not intended by the author.

No part of this book may be reproduced, or stored in a retrieval system, or transmitted in any form or by any means, electronic, mechanical, photocopying, recording, or otherwise, without express written permission of the publisher.

CONTENTS

Title Page
Copyright
Content Note   1
Prologue   2
Chapter 1   4
Chapter 2   10
Chapter 3   23
Chapter 4   36
Chapter 5   50
Chapter 6   59
Chapter 7   68
Chapter 8   85
Chapter 9   94
Chapter 10   102
Lucy's Epilogue   114
Aldrig's Epilogue   117
Keep Reading   119

Books In This Series	121
Books By This Author	127
Free Romance Novel	131

CONTENT NOTE

Potential trigger: assault attempt on the heroine by a secondary character. Everything ends well, but the scene can be triggering.

PROLOGUE

No one remembers the world before the Shift. It was thousands of years ago, all lost, all forgotten. Scientists and historians say that before, the world was better, brighter, and our planet belonged to us, humans. There were proud countries and bustling cities, and technology was at its highest.

We can hardly imagine all that. There is no proof, no written texts, no pictures of Alia Terra before the Shift. All we know is the face of Alia Terra now. The land haphazardly divided into territories, the walled cities, the poor living on the fringes, barely surviving.

The monsters.

The temples where young virgins can take a DNA test and be matched to one of them. An arranged marriage to a monster is often the only way a woman can save herself or give her family a chance to not starve.

This is Alia Terra. It belongs to the monsters, and we belong to them.

CHAPTER 1

Aldrig

"Thirteen hundred, fourteen hundred, fifteen hundred..." The priestess counted the money, letting the credits drop into a gold bowl on the altar. Each made a metallic clang, and I forced back a growl. In my current state of impatience, her slow, performative movements were especially irritating.

"Two thousand," she finally announced with a shallow bow that was purely ritualistic. Not a sign of respect. "The full sum. The temple thanks you for the prompt payment. You can be assured we will deal with it as promised."

I gritted my teeth, forcing myself not to look around. The large hall of glittering blue marble and golden fires bustled with subdued energy. People doing business, each at an altar similar to the one we stood by, everyone behaving with quiet reverence.

She would not be here, of course. My future mate, the human woman who was my genetic match, prepared for the wedding ceremony in one of the back chambers, hidden from view.

Even so, I had the urge to keep looking. Something told me I would recognize her at once, even though I had not seen her before. The temple didn't send out pictures of the arranged matches.

"Can you remind me what exactly was promised?" I asked, reining my instincts in. A few minutes of waiting would not make a difference now.

It was important to see a deal through to the end.

The priestess bowed, her impeccably curled hair sliding over her bare shoulders. She was tall for a human and held her spine rigid, even her bows seeming unyielding. Like all other priests in this temple, she wore a simple white toga tied with a golden belt.

Her clothes seemed unassuming but were actually of high quality. The temples were obscenely rich. Hence my question.

"But of course," the priestess said, her tone polite. "The temple will retain twenty-five percent of the sum for the processing costs of your request. The remaining sum will be transferred to your bride's designated relative as payment for her participation in the ceremony."

I scoffed, looking away from her cool face.

Participation in the ceremony. It meant my bride's relatives would be paid for her becoming my wife. For the hundredth time, I wondered about her reasons for being here.

Humans had only disdain and fear for us, giants from the north, creatures of cool blood and violent ways. I read pamphlets and books describing us as uncouth, barbaric, beastly. *Animals.* No human woman would have entered a union with one of us on her own, I was sure.

But there were plenty of those desperate enough to trade their virginity and life in return for bettering the lives of their relatives.

Her reasons didn't matter, ultimately. Once she was mine, I would do anything to make her want to stay.

"Good," I told the priestess, my voice and manners cooler than her own in my growing fury. "See to it that they receive the funds immediately."

"As soon as the ritual is complete," she said with another bow. It seemed mocking. "If you don't have any more questions, I will guide you to the wedding chamber. It has been prepared for you and your party."

I looked over my shoulder at Luca and Sveg, who gave me wide grins. Behind them, Ullag loomed, his face closed off.

I didn't want him here, but we shared one father, and Ullag held the most power apart from me. If I didn't invite him, he would be the first to question my unorthodox union with a human woman. He had to be here to see the ritual with his own eyes. The woman would belong to me, and any heirs she gave birth to would be mine.

Without a doubt.

"Lead the way," I told the priestess, quenching the new wave of fury that threatened to boil over.

Ullag was the reason I decided to get matched. I was the first ice giant to use the temple's services, and I was sure there already was much gossip about it back home.

Once I carried my bride into the palace, it would only get worse. People would whisper about how I defiled traditions and the customs of our forebears. They would wonder if a human woman could birth me a child.

And they would most definitely be curious about my reasons for picking a human mate when so many giant females would be too happy to lie with me and give me heirs.

We followed the priestess out of the main room with high ceilings and columns of gold-veined blue marble into a wide corridor lit with faux torches. Their fires were expert holograms, imitating the chaotic nature of fire without giving off smoke or heat.

The ritual we were about to perform was simple, a

ceremony from the olden times when we still lived in our world. Most ice giants didn't mate for life. We always had fewer females, and they had their pick of the males. Once a female gave birth to a male's child, she left it with the father and went on her way, looking for another male who would suit her fancy.

But kings used to take wives. It was the prerogative of the ruler and the way to keep the dynasty lines uncontested.

The ritual came from those times. A simple ceremony, vows said over a living fire, an exchange of bread and salt.

And a public consummation.

I gritted my teeth, feeling Ullag's presence behind me on a visceral level. Luca and Sveg walked in rhythm with me, their steps perfectly even, while Ullag's hit a beat later, his long strides out of sync. I wondered if he did it deliberately.

Brother or not, he was not my friend, and would always follow my lead with reluctance.

We dueled once. When our father died, and the funeral rites were performed, we fought for his legacy right in front of his pyre, as was customary. The outcome seemed obvious from the start. Ullag was bigger, older, more experienced.

And still, I won. Because I was faster, stronger, and more determined. I had our father's blessing, too. He couldn't designate an heir, as the crown had to be won in a duel. But he told us while lying on his deathbed.

"I hope Aldrig is king after me."

And so I became king. In revenge, Ullag seduced Rhiannon, who was my mate. A year later, when I took another mate, meaning to perform the ritual and have her be my wife, he lured her away, too.

I hadn't been with a female ever since. Five years it had been. Five long, lonely years, marred by a bitter resentment toward my brother—and fear of another humiliation.

This time, it would be different. The woman I was about to wed was my exact match. According to the temple and their science, she would bear me strong, healthy children. I would marry her in the sight of Ullag and my two brothers in arms, and she would be mine forever.

No one would lure her away.

The priestess stopped in front of a tall gilded door and turned to us.

"Your wedding chamber."

I opened the door and strode inside.

CHAPTER 2

Lucy

I stood in the middle of the opulent chamber, fretting. My lips were chapped, and I chewed on a loose bit of skin—a bad habit that would lead to bleeding if I didn't stop. With a sigh, I clenched my jaw, forcing a deep breath into my belly.
Soon. I would see him soon.

But the wait was excruciating. Before, there were things to occupy my attention. First, I had to travel from our village in the mountains to Tenuga, the nearest city. The cranky old train crawled through the forests and machine-operated fields, and even though it was much slower than the fancy hovercrafts the rich used, it was convenient enough.

I had never ridden on a train before. And I couldn't help but compare the convenient journey with the way I had to travel before I was matched to a monster.

We were too poor for trains, and on the rare occasions when we had to get to the city, we went on foot. The journey took three days.

Like when I went to give my blood sample at the temple. I walked all the way, propelled by the wild hope of being matched to someone. My only supplies were a bottle of water and a pack of dry bread to nibble on. My brother insisted I take some cheese, too, but Daisy was still malnourished, according to the village nurse.

Daisy was my youngest sister. She was four, and yet she looked like a two-year-old. Her eyes were so big in her small, sunken face.

I made her eat all the cheese before I left.

When I came back after giving my sample to the temple, I was so starved, I didn't feel hunger anymore.

Thankfully, they found my match almost at once. The letter came, announcing my destination, a train ticket attached. Of course, there was no information about who my match was. The temples never let you know in advance to prevent the matched brides from running away in fear.

An unknown monster was better than knowing one's fate for certain.

Because that's what he would be. A monster.

And yet, I wept for joy. There was no guarantee of being matched and receiving the compensation, so

I regarded it as a stroke of wild luck. Thanks to it, my brothers and sisters would be provided for. They would have money to buy a cow and a few chickens, and then they would finally have enough to eat.

Even now, although my heart hammered with anxiety in the blue and gold room, I smiled happily as the flame of relief rose in my chest.

They would be fine. Daisy would be fine. She wouldn't die of starvation like our cousin, Anna, and many others before her.

My becoming a matched bride turned our fate around. I didn't have to make another arduous journey to the city, because this time, I could get on a train. The journey that took three days on foot took three hours on the train.

The temple provided the ticket, food during the journey, and the clothes I now wore.

As soon as I boarded the train, I received a cup of broth and soft, fresh bread. An hour later, someone came over to refill my cup and gave me a bite of chicken meat. When I got off, I got another portion of food, slightly bigger.

They knew exactly how to feed someone on the brink of starvation. I was one of many desperate, half-dead brides who offered themselves in return for salvation for their families.

I traveled through a portal from the temple in Tenuga to the one where my future husband would be. There, they fed me again. After that, a priestess led me to a bath, where I was bathed three times in a row.

My long hair and nails were cut, my skin blasted with a machine I had never seen before that made it all dewy, and I was dressed in a soft, loose dress that hid my hard edges from view.

My hair was braided, my face lightly painted. When I saw myself in a gold-framed mirror, I gasped. The woman I saw was a stranger. She looked soft, even sophisticated, like women from the city when they went shopping.

Lost was her tough look of a grimy survivor. The girl who fought every day for scraps of food to feed her family was hidden from view. But it didn't mean she was gone.

The eyes gave me away. They looked dark and hungry, shining with the hard glint of determination.

And fear.

I could navigate the village market easily. I could draw a hard bargain, forcing a reluctant employer to pay my meager wages, or even hunt with a sling if I had to. But I didn't know how to be a bride, and it showed.

Get a grip.

The door clanged, and I whipped in place, clenching my fists. It had to be him. I would finally see him.

The price for the lives of my family. The monster who needed a human bride, a match arranged through a temple, because he could not find one himself.

Because he was, in all likelihood, damaged, or cruel, or ugly beyond belief.

My future.

I exhaled when a serving girl slipped inside, carrying a tray with two cups and plates.

"They will be here soon," she said with a cheerful smile, setting the tray on a table.

She lit a fire in a large metal bowl in the middle of the room. It caught at once, red flames leaping over dry wood and an artificial burning component, the chamber filling with a smell I couldn't identify. It was rich and woodsy, a bit like resin, and yet different enough that I couldn't pin it down.

I inhaled and held the fragrant breath in my lungs, my shoulders relaxing. The serving girl left, and I let out the breath and took in another.

So this was it. Whatever would happen now, at least the wait was almost over. I would see him. I would know.

And I knew, as I had known all along, that whoever, *whatever*, he was, I would not turn back. I could still say no, of course. But I would not. This was the only way I could save my brothers and sisters, and as I was the oldest in the family now that our parents were dead, it was my duty.

I would do whatever I had to.

That thought gave me the courage to face the one piece of furniture in the glorious wedding chamber that I avoided. I turned to it now, taking in the gilded frame, the furs and satin sheets draped over the large mattress, the luxurious pillows.

I knew, of course, that some races required immediate consummation of a marriage. In my naivety, I hoped my match would have a different custom, but of course, luck was not on my side anymore.

I hoped that he would at least belong to one of the smaller races, like elves and some aliens, but my cynicism turned that hope into cinders. I learned long ago to prepare for the worst possible outcome—because that, at least, helped you survive.

If my luck held, he would be the biggest of them all.

Not only would I have my first time with a stranger, he would also be so big, he could rip me in half.

I laughed a small, bubbling laugh that grew and grew, filling my belly with butterflies, making me lightheaded. I tried to stop myself, but I only laughed harder and harder, hysteria gripping me completely.

Not good. I had to do the ritual. Only then would my family receive the money. I needed to get a grip.

The door opened again, the metallic sound cutting my laughter off. Again, the same serving girl. She gave me a shallow bow and another smile, and set a crystal pitcher of something golden on the table by the bed.

"The virgin oil," she said with another cheerful smile. "Apply before penetration. It will make everything go smoothly. Good luck!"

This time, I didn't dare laugh for fear of not being able to stop. I looked at the pitcher, my anxiety foaming up my belly and chest. Apply before penetration... This wasn't a standard practice as far as I knew. They only brought the oil when there was a significant size difference. Which meant...

Oh dear gods.

I strode over to the pitcher and grabbed it, sniffing. It smelled pleasant, like apricots and cinnamon, and I cast a worried look at the doorway. Should I just apply it now? Or should I wait? Would there be time? Would my future husband wait for me? Or would he just...

The door opened again, and I gasped, hastily setting the pitcher aside and hiding my hands behind my back.

I turned, my mouth half open, ready to greet him or apologize, or...

The strangest creature I ever saw walked through the door, ducking his head. *Dear gods.* The doorway was too low for him. Though it was high enough that it could fit me with another person sitting on my shoulders.

He had to duck to go through.

My mouth dried, and I took a step back, my hip jamming into the corner of a bedside table. Any words I had ready on my tongue dispersed and sunk into a paralysis of terror that gripped me from the inside, making my breathing shallow, my hands clammy.

As if through dense water, I watched as he slowly straightened, the top of his head brushing the ceiling.

Merciful gods.

He wasn't just tall. That alone, I could have accepted, seeing as there were races of various kinds and sorts on Alia Terra, and I was used to seeing some of them.

But my groom was massive in a way that brought shivers down my spine and into my belly. He was broad in the shoulders, his limbs as thick and sturdy as tree trunks. Muscles rippled down his torso and arms, and his stomach looked unnaturally chiseled.

I kept staring, propriety and manners forgotten as I took him in, my instincts jumping from detail to detail, assessing the danger.

He looked *hard*. Inhumanly hard, with sharp edges, as if his body were part-flesh, part-stone. The effect was made only more powerful by the bluish-gray color of his skin. This man was part stone, and everything about him was strong, unyielding, and somehow... cold.

I wasn't ready to look at his face, so I looked further down. He wore leather trousers, though his chest was bare. They sat low on his hips, and even from the other side of the spacious room, I clearly saw the bulge between his legs.

So that was why they gave me the oil. I doubted it would be of any help.

His legs were as powerful as the rest of him, and suddenly, I had a vivid image of him picking up an enormous boulder as if it weighed nothing and throwing it far, far ahead.

A killing machine.

"When you're ready, Lucy," came a cool female voice. I jerked my head away and noticed the priestess, one I hadn't seen yet, standing next to my future husband.

She was taller than me, and yet the top of her head barely reached past his waist.

Oh gods and fates.

And this... this... giant... was supposed to be my husband? Forever?

A small giggle burst like a bubble in my throat, making me cough. Not forever. I wouldn't live through this ritual, because if he impaled me on his cock, I would die.

I took another critical look at his bulge, and another

word came unbidden, helping me categorize him and put what I saw into thought.

He was *virile.* So very male, I trembled from his presence. Something fluttered in my belly, the nausea turning into an insistent, hot pulse, and I sighed, stepping from foot to foot.

Maybe I would at least die happy.

Come on, Lu. You can do it. For Daisy.

I took a deep breath and looked all the way up, craning my neck so I could see his face looming under the high ceiling.

The air rushed out of me in a surprised gasp, and I stared without blinking, completely taken aback.

I expected him to look savage. I imagined sharp, rotting teeth, unkempt hair, ears torn from barbaric fighting, and ruthless eyes with no soul.

But there were none of those things.

The skin on his face was more blue than gray, and though it had the same cold, stony look to it, his expression was soft. Deep lines marred his face, darker shadows pooling under his cheek bones, and his mouth was closed, full lips forming a thoughtful expression.

He had a strong nose, wide and straight, and it somehow made his face look noble. His features were proportional, and his eyes…

"Oh," I said, finally regaining my ability to speak.

"Hello."

His eyes shone an electric blue, so bright they seemed magical. And as soon as I looked into them, I knew.

He was not a beast. He was a person.

He didn't reply. His eyes were fixed on my face with an intensity that made me blush. I looked away, feeling utterly exposed. He watched me as if he could see through my clothes, through the layers of skin, to my very heart and mind.

And I felt so vulnerable without my usual armor of dirt, rags, and hidden weapons.

A movement caught my eye. Three more bluish giants walked inside, and my breath caught in my throat. The last one was the biggest of them all, and he had a look of cold menace on his face as he eyed me slowly. I shuffled again, stepping from foot to foot, gripping the soft fabric of my dress in my clammy hands.

Who were they? And which one was my groom?

I flicked my gaze back to the first giant, begging the fates that it would be him. Because if I were to choose, he was the one I would pick, the big bulge be damned. Something about him made me feel… not safe, exactly.

He just didn't seem like a complete stranger.

"Perfect," the priestess said, her voice serene. "Now that we are all here, let us proceed. Lucy, come to the altar."

She motioned at the metal bowl of fragrant fire in the middle of the room. I swallowed thickly around a lump in my throat and went. My steps were slow but sure, and I felt strangely disconnected from my body. As if my legs walked on their own, out of my control.

I stopped by the altar, still gripping my dress to hide the trembling of my hands.

"Aldrig," the priestess said.

I cocked my head to the side, wondering what it meant, when the giant, the one who came in first, the one with sentient eyes blazing blue, moved forward, stopping opposite me.

His name, I guessed.

So it was him. And he was called Aldrig. I whispered it under my breath, trying his name out, almost tasting it. It felt good on my tongue. Easy to pronounce. Smooth.

I looked up, and a fresh wave of apprehension slid down my back. When we stood close by, only the fire altar between us, he seemed even more massive. Like a small mountain looming over me.

And he didn't look at me. His eyes were fixed on his companions, a savage look on his face, his white teeth bared, upper lip pulled back.

I flinched, my relief that it was him dissipating at once. But as his eyes went back to me, his face softened, and he closed his mouth.

"Hello, Lucy."

I shivered. His voice was deep, so deep it brought to mind hidden caves, or the force of avalanches crashing down mountainsides.

It reverberated in my chest and belly, and I bit back a whimper. I was so high strung, every sensation felt immediate and electrifying. Whatever happened next, I would feel everything keenly.

"Join hands over the fire," the priestess said, standing on my right, while the three other giants shuffled to the space on my left, stopping a distance away from us.

Spectators.

I stifled another whimper and didn't allow myself to wonder if they were here to see the entire ceremony. Whatever happened, I would get through this.

For Daisy.

Yes. I would do anything for my brothers and sisters. That was why I was here. So they would not be hungry anymore.

And yet, as the giant's icy hand enveloped my trembling one, I couldn't help but cringe.

So cold. So hard.

So alien.

CHAPTER 3

Aldrig

Her hand was so small and fragile in mine, I held it with utmost care. It felt like one careless move, one thoughtless action, and I would crush the delicate woman trembling before me.

When I first saw her, I felt a mix of awe and dismay. She seemed precious and perfect, her skin warmed by a blush, her eyes big and alert, brimming with emotions. And yet...

So small. How would I ever fit inside her? How would she be able to bear my children?

The temples swore by their genetic matches. According to their database, this woman would fit me perfectly, despite her small frame and narrow hips.

I quashed the worry and trusted the science. She was my bride, and I had to admit, I was proud to be matched with such a sweet, genteel-looking female. She was so unlike the strong, ham-fisted females of my race. A giantess didn't need a male to protect her. She went where she wished, leaving behind her a trail of broken hearts and unwanted children.

This woman would need me. She would stay by my side and rely on me, and our children would not be left motherless.

She was like a rare gem. A prized possession.

Yes, I was proud and eager. I would own her for my brothers to see, and I would make sure there was no doubt she enjoyed it.

And if the temple science was wrong... we would find out soon enough.

Still, when I saw how afraid she was, how truly small against me, another seed of doubt prickled deep in my gut. Was she really as skittish as she looked? Would I be doomed to a life of deliberate movements, soft-spoken words, and holding all my instincts in check?

All I wanted was to lay her open on the sacrificial bed and feast on her, and then claim her for all to see. I didn't want to be gentle and patient. I wanted to flood her with my seed, make her overflow with it, planting my heirs inside her womb.

But as I looked down at the woman whose head didn't even reach my waist, the doubt deepened, turning into unease. A genetic match was all fine and well, but what of our personalities? I knew nothing about her, and she knew nothing about me.

Would we even be able to hold a conversation? Would she be my equal, a comfort, and a supportive spouse like I planned to be for her?

Or would she only do her duties and nothing more, like a broodmare?

I was about to take a step back, my doubts making me hesitant.

But at that exact moment, she looked up, her eyes flaming with determination. Her mouth was set in a line, and I realized her appearance was deceptive. The delicate body hid a creature of strength and grit, one who looked at me with fierce courage.

I smiled, some of my worries alleviated. After a moment, she smiled back, her eyes never leaving my face.

If she had some fire, we would make this work. I was sure of it.

"Let us begin," the priestess said, and I stroked down the inside of Lucy's wrist with my thumb.

Her eyes widened, and she shivered, but it didn't seem like it was from fear. I stroked again, applying a bit more pressure. Her skin was deliciously warm, and I couldn't imagine what it would feel like to kiss and caress her. To be inside…

Ice giants were cool, in and out. To plunge into her hot body… I hardened at the thought, dark desire stirring in my loins.

"Repeat after me, Lucy," the priestess said, turning to my bride.

She nodded. Her eyes never left mine as she said the vow, repeating every few words after the priestess, her voice strong and determined.

"I, Lucy Mano, stand before you as your bride. I welcome you to my body and soul, to my life and my future, and vow to belong to you forever, as you will belong to me. I give you my obedience, faithfulness, and my heart."

She looked into my eyes while speaking those words, and my instincts stirred, growing in power, until my entire body thrummed with the need to claim her now, to protect her, to give her everything so she would be happy forever.

Lucy's voice didn't crack until the last line of the vow.

"I give myself to you, Aldrig, the k-king of ice giants."

She looked surprised and a little scared as she repeated my title after the priestess. And yet, her eyes never left my face, apprehension soon melting into awe.

I knew my vow by heart, and before the priestess asked me to repeat after her, I said it in full.

"I, Aldrig, the king of ice giants, stand before you as your groom. I offer you my body and my soul, my life and my future, and vow to belong to you forever, as you will belong to me. I give you my protection, my home, and my heart. I take you as my wife, Lucy Mano."

The priestess nodded and turned to a table, on which a tray of bread and salt was left. Two metal plates, on each a bite of dark bread, and two cups filled with the dark, bluish salt mined on our lands.

"You will now feed each other bread and salt as the symbol of the duties of husband and wife that you vow to perform."

I took a piece of bread and pressed it into the salt. I turned it up, taking a moment to admire how the blue crystals shimmered in the light of the fire.

"The wife eats at her husband's table and opens her body to welcome his seed," the priestess said.

Lucy blushed, a delicious red stain spreading over her cheeks. When I brought the bread to her lips, I felt the heat of her blush against my knuckles.

She opened her mouth, and I put the bread inside, letting my finger brush against her lips. I hissed, the wet heat of her skin sending a thrill into me as Lucy's blue eyes turned up, giving me a look I couldn't decipher.

She closed her mouth, chewing quickly, and swallowed, the movement of her throat pronounced.

"Your turn," I said, watching her without blinking.

All my instincts and senses were now trained on her,

and the rest of the room blurred and disappeared in shadow as my bride filled my vision. I heard nothing but her quick, nervous breaths, the thumping of her heart, the susurration of her dress brushing against the altar.

I inhaled, trying to pick her fragrance out of the many scents mixing in the room. There was the smoke, the priestess, my brothers. And something sweet, a faint note that came from the bed. And then...

Her. She smelled human, but clean and fresh. Her scent had a sharp edge, slightly acidic, and a warm note underneath. Something spicy, which felt like it would burn if I tasted it.

With trembling fingers, she picked up the piece of bread and pressed it into the dish of salt, just as I did. She raised her hand, and I lowered my head, knowing she wouldn't be able to reach my mouth if I stood tall.

I bent over the fire, capturing her fingers between my lips. She gasped, and I ran my tongue over her warm skin, letting her taste mingle with that of the salt and bread, all three combining into the flavor of my future.

"The husband receives the children that his wife shall give him and provides for his family."

I released Lucy's fingers after running my tongue over them and cherishing their warmth. Then I straightened, swallowing the bread she fed me.

"The official part of the ceremony is over," the priestess said, all business. "Congratulations. You have the use of this chamber until the evening. I wish you a long, happy marriage."

She gave us each a polite smile and turned away. Lucy's mouth fell open, her eyes wide, and she took a few steps after the priestess, but she was already out of the chamber, the door closing. Lucy stopped, breathing hard, and dropped her head.

Sveg and Luca whooped and came over to pat me on the back. Ullag shuffled after them and shook my hand briefly, giving me a nod. But despite the polite gesture, I saw the challenge in his eyes.

He would try to take her away from me, I knew.

And I would do anything to keep her. Starting now.

"Thank you," I told the giants. "Now stay away and bear witness."

"You break her in well," Luca said with a wide grin.

"Oh, I will," I said, looking directly at Ullag. "I'll make sure she's all mine."

Without another word, I turned to Lucy, whose face was bright red. I walked over, only two steps taking me close, and gently traced my fingers down her cheek. We gasped together, she from surprise and I from the heat of the blush pulsing under her cheeks.

Gods. I could not wait.

And yet, I knew I had to.

"Wait," she said, her voice high-pitched. "They gave me. Um. Oil. To apply before… penetration. So if you could just turn away, I will quickly…"

"Lucy," I interrupted her frantic speech, taking her wringing hands into mine. "We have time. Please, don't fear me."

Her eyes flashed away to my brothers standing under a wall by the door, far away from the bed, yet with a good view of it.

"They will stay," I said, trying to make my voice soothing, though judging by her flinching, I failed. "It's customary. My brothers will bear witness so no one can contest that you are my wife."

She looked back at me, her eyes wide, nostrils flared with quick, fearful breaths.

"We don't usually… do that in public…" She trailed off, turning her hands in my grip.

I took her palm and lifted it gently. Slowly, looking at her the entire time, I bent low and ran my lips over the inner side of her wrist. She shivered, her already big eyes growing larger, and I kissed that warm place, feeling her wild pulse beating against my lips.

Lucy took a shivering breath and watched me. I trailed my lips up her forearm, planting kisses on her skin until I reached the crease of her elbow, and I swiped my tongue over the hot, delicate skin.

She let out a small sound. It didn't sound like a moan an aroused giantess would make, and yet it traveled straight to my cock, already straining against the fabric of my trousers.

"It's only this once," I said, looking up. Her face was so close and so tiny. She looked adorable with the blushing cheeks and red lips parted in emotion.

I wanted to see what expression she would make when I entered her.

"And I'll make sure you forget they are even here," I whispered, letting my cool breath envelop her face until she shivered.

Without giving her time to fret any longer, I caught her hair, ever so gently, and tilted her head back. Still bent low over her, I slanted my lips against hers.

I hissed from the impact. Her mouth was small compared to mine, but soft and scalding. I moved my lips against her warm skin, the kiss slow and exploratory at first.

As my lips slid over hers, looking for the point when the kiss would feel natural, I ran my hands up her back, marveling at how I covered almost the entire expanse of it with both palms.

Lucy gasped, a hot breath warming my cool skin, and then she kissed me back.

I froze, my fingers splayed wide over her back, my lips moving gently to adjust to her rhythm. She tasted spicy, and my cock throbbed, because the heat of her, the softness, fed something dark and hungry inside me that I didn't even realize was there.

A cold, gaping cave that was suddenly exposed and brought to light. And she was that light, a warm flame shining over the walls, and showing me how truly lonely I was.

That new hunger driving me on, I gripped her buttocks with one hand and hoisted her up. She gasped into my mouth as I brought her to my height, holding her close as I pressed my tongue against her lower lip, making her open her mouth.

I pushed inside, swallowing her gasp, and stroked her tongue with mine. As I tasted the fiery heat, I couldn't help but thrust my hips, my still hidden cock yearning to taste it, too. To plunge deep into the marvelous, hot cunt of my bride.

She struggled against me, and I slowed, alarm piercing through my haze. Was she hurt? Did I do something…

But no. She didn't struggle to get away. Her small palms found purchase over my bare shoulders, blunt nails digging into my skin, and she put her legs around me, gasping when she realized my torso was too broad for her to grip me with her thighs.

That was good. She already gave in to my touch, forgetting about my brothers. But I would not forget. Even now, I glanced at Ullag from the corner of my eye, making sure he noticed.

I would make her scream from pleasure, and he would have to listen.

My bride behaved exactly as I needed her to, and she didn't even require instruction. I brought her closer with a sound of appreciation, devouring her mouth while I shuffled my forearm under her butt, supporting her better so she could be more comfortable. I ran my other hand up her exposed leg, bare skin revealed where the dress rode up.

Warm and smooth. I made another sound, something demanding and impatient, and she dragged her nails down the back of my head, leaving tingles in the wake of her touch.

I walked to the bed and laid her down on the mattress, spreading her legs open. She gasped and tried to sit up, her blushing face losing its delicious, unfocused expression.

"The oil," she said, pointing at a bedside table. "Please, I have to…"

"I remember," I said, running my palm up her inner thigh.

Gods, she was so small. My hand encompassed her entire thigh at its widest point. I glanced at the oil again, committing it to memory.

Since this was supposed to make sex with me easier on her, she would drip with the oil before I fucked her.

"And I will not fuck you just yet," I said, looking at her face. She looked so vulnerable, with eyes wide open and glistening. "I am going to taste you."

She opened her mouth to speak, but only a strangled sound came out. I grinned and dove to the junction of her thighs, spreading her legs wider yet.

She didn't have underwear on.

For a moment, I only looked at her. So similar... And yet so different.

Her skin here was dark red. It glistened with arousal, and as I pressed my face closer, watching her small opening and wondering how in the world my cock would fit inside, the heat of her slid down my skin.

I didn't touch her yet, and still the air between us buzzed with the warmth she gave off.

I closed my eyes and inhaled, letting my tongue out to taste her scent, letting the heat penetrate into me.

Intoxicating and bewitching, her smell spiraled up my nose and into my brain, making my thoughts fire up and focus on one prerogative.

To breed. And breed so well she would swell with my child in no time. So that Ullag would always know. Whatever he tried, her firstborn would be only mine.

I stroked my cock through my trousers, gritting my teeth at how uncomfortable it felt not to be inside her now.

Her very scent made my body light up in response. The warmth of her skin, which should have been uncanny, turned my arousal up so much, I could barely think. It didn't matter that she was human, and it didn't matter that she was smaller than half of me, that Ullag was plotting.

Only one thing mattered: that I take her and make her mine beyond contestation.

But no. I had to be slow. And remember the oil.

At least I could satisfy some of my hunger.

CHAPTER 4

Lucy

I couldn't hold back a loud moan when his cool tongue slid over me.
Merciful gods.

It seemed unreal, completely impossible. He was a stranger, a monster, a giant so big, my mind had trouble processing it. And yet...

And yet I squirmed as he tasted me. I squirmed, making appalling, encouraging sounds, and wished... for more.

A fire burned in my belly, arousal so strong it would have felt unpleasant if he wasn't doing such a great job alleviating it. Every lick of his cold tongue soothed the heat while also turning it up.

My legs were spread so wide, my muscles aching with it, but he held me firmly, and soon, the ache faded away. There was only the delightful, uncanny pleasure building up in my core. I squeezed my eyes shut, cutting off the marble ceiling and the dancing shadows cast by the fire on the altar.

I cut everything off and focused only on his hard grip against my thighs and the cool pressure over my pussy and clit. The coldness of his touch was shocking still, but now, it also sent wicked prickles of pleasure through me.

When he fitted his mouth over my entire core and plunged his tongue inside, I cried out, my body tensing. His tongue was big like everything else about him, and the stretch of it burned…

And then it didn't. The cold soothed the pain, and as he pulled his tongue out and pushed it back into me, I gasped from how good it felt.

Out of this world.

I had never been with a man, too busy working to provide for my family even when my parents were still alive. There was no time for romance, and the thought of getting pregnant and bringing another child into our poverty stifled any other urges I might have had.

Except now, begetting a child would make my place at Aldrig's side certain. And giving myself over to my husband meant my family would be saved.

As Aldrig's tongue slid in and out of me, cold, hard, and relentless, I floated in a strange place where my body felt light and alive. It buzzed with pleasure, and every cold stroke made the sensation more powerful until all I could do was shake and whimper, overwhelmed by the pressure building inside me.

I had *some* experience, having played with myself in the rare moments I was alone, but this... This was something completely different. The cold of his touch somehow reined me in, which meant the tension kept building without release.

Every flick of his tongue, every teasing lick and thrust strung me higher until it felt like nothing existed but my body and me trapped inside, devoid of control.

Finally, it felt like something inside me would give, would snap any moment, and I...

Aldrig stopped and straightened, his face high over me.

"Please," I whispered, uncertain what I asked for. All I knew was the disappointment coursing through me.

He smiled, white teeth flashing in his blue face, the color of his skin more intense. I blushed when I saw how his mouth glistened.

Aldrig grabbed the pitcher of oil without getting up, his long arm reaching easily. I made to raise myself, but he pressed my stomach down, giving me a cautionary look.

"Stay."

A quiet laughter resounded from the other side

of the room, and I remembered we weren't alone. How did I forget? Here I lay, completely open with everything on display, while those other giants saw everything, and…

A cool, wet touch between my labia broke my train of thought. I gasped, raising myself on my forearms so I could see, and shoved the awareness that the others were here out of my mind.

Aldrig poured the oil over my core, and the gold, unctuous potion splashed over me, sliding down to my butthole and pooling under me on the sheets.

"It's… messy…" I said weakly, because I didn't truly mind.

Aldrig grunted in response and put the pitcher away. I was all wet and sticky, and the oil coated my swollen skin, glistening. The sensation made a new wave of heat rush through me, and my insides clenched expectantly.

Something else happened, too. My core warmed pleasantly and relaxed, the tension seeping out. Suddenly, I felt much more open and more pliant, and a wave of pleasure washed over my pelvis.

"Oh."

Aldrig looked up, a frown on his forehead. He ran his fingers over me, tips gently swirling in the oil, while his eyes focused on my face.

"Oh!" I said again, mouth open while I panted. "It feels…"

But I couldn't finish, because he found my opening and slowly, so very slowly, pushed his finger in my pussy.

I closed my eyes and pressed my lips together, and yet I couldn't hold in the loud moan of pleasure.

His finger was cold and hard, and as it pushed the oil into me, my body alighted with warm, overwhelming pleasure. I shuddered as he pushed further in, and as he opened me, the very first penetration making way inside me, I felt how my body gave way.

"You are so warm," he murmured, and I looked at his face through my lashes.

His mouth was open like mine, quick breaths cool over my skin, and his eyes were dark, all pupil and almost no iris.

Suddenly, I realized we were supposed to be making love, the both of us, and yet I only lay here and let him caress me without touching him in return. I bit my lip, unsure of myself, and tried to sit up.

"Should I also… touch you?" I asked, cringing at how stupid I probably sounded.

But he shook his head, pulling his finger out of me. He swirled it over me again, gathering more oil and teasing my clit, and I whimpered, fighting to keep my eyes open. They closed against my will as pleasure overwhelmed me.

"We have time," he murmured, pushing the finger

back in until I shuddered from the uncanny bliss of feeling his cold touch against my inflamed skin. "Right now, I want to worship my bride and learn what pleases her."

My eyes flashed open in surprise. I looked at him, confused, and he grinned, removing his finger again and reaching for the pitcher of oil. He poured more over me, and as the tingling warmth seeped into my skin, relaxing me further, he chuckled.

"Don't worry, little snowflake," he whispered, his voice so low only I could hear it. "I will take my pleasure from you soon enough."

Instead of dread, which would be the appropriate emotion, excitement fluttered in my belly. I truly didn't have to do anything. Didn't have to worry, or perform, and fight for his attention.

All I had to do was lie there and allow him to touch me.

With a sigh, I lay back, and when his finger slid into me again, easy now in the slick, I raised my hips to pull him in deeper.

"That's right," he said quietly, pushing further in. "Just like this, little snowflake."

I moaned as coldness spread over my core when his finger pushed all the way in, his knuckles pressing against me.

"You're doing very well."

He pulled his finger out, pouring more oil onto me,

and pushed back in...

I cried out. It was more, more hard coldness making its way inside, more painful stretching that had me instinctively closing my thighs.

But he didn't stop, only kept pushing, and after a moment of discomfort, my body gave. I relaxed, the warmth of the oil filling me just as the cold of his fingers soothed the burn.

Fingers, because I realized there were two.

When his knuckles pressed into me, I opened my eyes and mouth in wonder. His palms were massive! One finger was probably as thick as three of mine, not to even mention their length... And two whole fingers were inside me?

"We'll have to see about getting more of this oil," he said, pulling back.

More slick warmth gushed over me, and he pushed his fingers in my pussy in one, long stroke. I gasped, feeling completely full and utterly conquered, my body accommodating the girth of the invasion without any resistance.

Even though some doubts and apprehension still floated through my head, my body welcomed him fully, giving in so easily it was embarrassing.

"My beautiful bride," he said just as I clenched around him, the uncomfortable thought making me tighten. "You are taking this so well. I can't wait to be inside you."

I released with a deep breath, his words comforting. He praised me. Actually praised me, and it felt as warm as the oil, only not in my pussy, but in my chest.

Unbidden tears gathered in my eyes. He called me beautiful. Said I was doing well.

I couldn't remember the last time someone said something so kind to me.

"T-thank you," I croaked out, my voice wet with the unshed tears, which I valiantly tried to hold back. It didn't seem right for a bride to cry when her groom was about to fuck her.

He looked up, amused eyes locking with mine.

"Do not thank me for speaking the truth."

I nodded, transfixed by his dark eyes, and he fucked me slowly with his fingers amidst wet sounds that should have been embarrassing but weren't. They attested to how easily he could move inside me.

Aldrig pushed his fingers all the way in and looked down. I followed his gaze and gasped when I saw my belly.

There, under my skin, was a long, slightly protruding shape. We both saw his fingers inside me. I thought such a thing was impossible, or very painful at least, but it did not hurt. All I felt was the pleasure from the warmth mixing with the cold, and from the friction as he moved inside me.

He pulled his fingers out, and the bulge disappeared.

He pushed them back in, slowly… I saw the movement through my skin and muscle, seeing him moving inside me.

"You are ready, snowflake," he said, his voice guttural.

With one sharp tug, he tore my dress in half, baring my stomach and torso. I squeaked, trying to cover myself with the torn halves of the dress, and he put his hand over mine.

"I'll get you a hundred dresses. But now, I have to see you."

I let my hands fall to the sides, and he just looked at me, eyes glued to my breasts.

My face colored in shame. I knew men liked big-chested women, but I was so undernourished, my tits were barely there. I turned my eyes away, biting my lip, and Aldrig grunted.

"Fuck. I can't wait any longer."

I looked up, startled. He stared at my red nipples, his mouth in a tight line. Apparently, my breasts didn't turn him off, which was a relief.

Without looking away, he stood up and stepped out of his trousers.

Oh dear.

I gaped. Was I impressed that my body accommodated two of his fingers? Did I feel relieved? Well, now I was back to panicking, because my groom's cock was gigantic.

And not only that. I had seen human cocks when other kids at school brought porn magazines, and we all had a good look and a laugh until a very flushed teacher confiscated them.

Aldrig's cock was very unlike the human ones.

For one, it was a deep blue, and the skin had a hard, stony look to it. Girthier at the base than at the tip, it curved upward, its shape a bow rather than a rod.

Thick, veiny lines ran up the length, crisscrossing and meandering without a clear pattern. They converged at the tip. At the point of convergence, there was a small circular opening, and it seeped a clear, translucent liquid that was tinged a light violet.

The opening pulsed, as did the veiny lines. As I watched, more liquid fell out, splashing on the mattress between my legs.

I looked up, my face most likely etched in horror, and found Aldrig watching me intently with an intense expression.

"Let's see if you can melt me with your heat," he said, his voice so low it vibrated.

I scooted back, giving him space on the huge bed. He crawled onto it, the mattress dipping dramatically under his weight. As he moved closer, sliding his massive thigh between mine, the bed gave a loud creak.

"Gotta tell them their furniture is crap," came a grumbling voice from the other side of the room.

One of the other ice giants. I closed my eyes and bit my lip, pushing back a sob trapped in my throat. It was too much. That huge cock, the heavy giant who would soon be on top of me, and his brothers watching everything…

Too much.

"Easy," Aldrig said, a cool touch ghosting over my cheek as he caressed it lightly with his finger. "Let's take this slowly. One bit at a time."

I nodded, and he slid further up my body. Now his immense, stony chest was right over me while his cock was positioned between my legs. I felt the cold hardness pressing into my inner thigh and swallowed thickly, readying myself for the pain.

Yet when Aldrig cautiously moved over me, all he did was press his cock into my clit and drag it over back and forth until a burst of pleasure helped me relax a bit. He grunted, the sound strained, and carefully moved over me.

I looked to the side and up, watching his arm. His powerful muscles were taut and bunched under his skin. Moving so cautiously cost him a great deal of effort.

He tried so hard. For me.

He pulled back slowly, dragging his cock over me one last time. I gave a long sigh, telling my body to soften, and reached down, gently wrapping my fingers around his shaft. They wouldn't go all the way around, and yet my light touch made Aldrig hiss and curse. I let go, startled, and he cursed again.

"Take it," he said, his voice a dangerous growl. "Guide me into you."

I gripped him again, with more certainty now, and pulled him to me. It took me a moment until I lined him up. All the while, he hovered above, his body like a roof over me, immovable and strong.

I gave his cold, hard cock a tug, wishing for this to be done. Because I expected pain, yes. But also… I was curious. A part of me wondered what it would feel like to be so stretched, so *full…*

Aldrig pushed in. One gasp from me, a groan from him, and the head of his cock was inside me. The cold felt electrifying, and I pulsed around him, my body reacting to the penetration.

But it didn't hurt. There was a stretching sensation, and the cold was at once pleasurable and uncomfortable. But there was no pain.

"You good, snowflake?" Aldrig asked in a growl.

"Um, yes."

"Good. Because if I don't fuck you soon, I'm going to explode."

I giggled, but my giggle turned into a loud gasp when he slid further in. *Merciful gods.* He moved slowly deeper, and I felt his progress keenly. He stretched me open, inch by inch, and I pulsed around him, my pussy stuffed so full, it had to be impossible…

And yet, he kept going. I reached between our bodies and felt for the place where we were joined. My skin there was taut and smooth to the touch, stretched to its limits. And his cock was… still mostly out of me.

I ran my fingers up with a shaky breath. A half of him was inside as far as I could tell. And already it felt like he reached my limit, so how…

There was a sharp pain deep inside me, and I cried out, which made him stop immediately.

"Too much?" he asked, voice tense.

"Yes," I answered, gulping deep breaths. "I'm sorry, but… no deeper."

"Don't be sorry," he said in a low voice and slowly pulled out.

Then he thrust back in, stopping at the right moment. I gasped as the cold length of him dragged over my sensitive inner places, his cold burning and adding to the sensation.

I put my hand on my belly and gasped when I felt the wide shape of him moving inside. As he drew out and pushed back in, I felt the exact place he reached with my fingers.

I closed my eyes and moaned as he thrust faster, moving in long, even strokes. I was stuffed full of huge, monster cock, and now that I got used to it, I felt all of it.

How he filled me to the brim, leaving no space for anything else. I felt the way he conquered me, pushing himself into my body, making way for himself with every stroke. His grunts made me blush with awe, because I was the source of his pleasure, and it felt good to hear those sounds.

I moaned out loud when he thrust faster yet, the friction sending violent jolts of ecstasy into me. And then…

His hips pressed the closest yet, settling against my inner thighs, and he stilled. I gasped as understanding dawned. He wasn't only halfway in anymore. He was… deep.

With a trembling hand, I touched my belly. The bulging shape was much further up. And all I felt was a wild satisfaction, and the greedy pulses of my pussy hugging him from all sides.

"We match after all," Aldrig said quietly. "My queen."

CHAPTER 5

Aldrig

Holding myself back from thrusting in abandon was the hardest thing I had ever done. My bride's body, so warm and responsive, already had me practically powerless. I wanted nothing more than to fuck her again and again until all my responsibilities, nay, the entire world, disappeared.

She would be sore and dripping with my cum, and still, I would want more.

Yet now, I clenched my teeth, my body so tense it would soon shake. Slow, measured strokes. In and out. Her mewls guided me, delicious sounds of her surrender and pleasure. It was the only thing that kept me in check.

To give my bride pleasure and not pain was more important than taking her as fast as I wanted. Her pleasure was more important than mine.

Because I would have her come apart for me. I would have her fully sated, her body coming all over my cock.

And Ullag would see.

I shoved away the thought of Ullag, growling at myself. Suddenly, with me and my bride so intimately joined, with her writhing under me in pleasure, it felt wrong to think about anyone but us.

I was inside, ensconced in her tight heat, practically foaming at the mouth with how good she made me feel. There was no space left between us for anyone else.

"Yes, like this," she breathed when I pulled almost completely out, my curved length dragging over the upper side of her pussy. "Oh gods. Please."

I slammed back into her, her heat scalding me, and pulled back just as I did before. She keened, a high-pitched sound, arching her back. I thrust hard, groaning with pleasure, too. I was seconds from coming inside her, but I had to hold back.

She would come first.

I pulled back again, the loss of her heat like a punch to the gut, and thrust fast, so deep my hips ground against her soft thighs.

She raised herself on the bed, her spine arching so high her bulging belly brushed against my skin. She was silent now, but I felt it.

My bride tightened around me like a vise, the

pressure making me grunt with the effort of holding myself back. She squeezed… and squeezed… until she finally released, her pleasure coming in rapid waves as she loosened and tightened around me.

She let out a deep groan, followed by a low moan.

There was a rushing sound in my ears, as if an icy wind, and through it, I vaguely heard the sounds of applause. My brothers noticed my bride came all over my cock and celebrated.

I didn't care. All I wanted now was to let go.

I fucked her hard, so hard, she slid up the bed. My every thrust was met with a strangled moan, her pussy so hot around me it burned, and yet…

With a loud groan, I came inside her, the orgasm pulling at my balls and some place deep within my pelvis, tightening and tightening. My cum shot out in long spurts, each one tugging harder, until I shook over my bride, my body locked in pleasure.

Finally, it eased, and with my last bit of strength, I rolled off her. My arms would no longer hold me up, but I didn't want to crush her, so I rolled.

Right onto the floor.

As I landed with a grunt of pain, the bed gave an ominous creak, shaking. Lucy shrieked in alarm, and a moment later, the shaking bed broke apart under her. She cried out when the mattress fell, no longer supported by the frame, and then she laughed.

I turned to find her dark, laughing eyes trained on me, and I grinned back, even though my body was killing me. There was a cramp in my thigh, and my arms felt too weak to raise. My cock, now limp and heavy over my thigh, felt as if it would never get hard again.

No wonder. This was the best sex and the most intense orgasm of my life.

"You good?" I asked Lucy, laughing quietly with her.

"Never better," she replied with a grin. "Though it feels like there's a puddle between my legs."

I raised my head with a grunt of effort. A pretty big puddle, indeed. My cum was still trickling out of her, but the majority was out, glistening on the sheets and slowly seeping into the mattress.

The sight made me swell with possessive pride. Here it was, the proof for all to see. This female was mine, and my seed was inside her, ready to grow into a baby.

"They charge an arm and a leg for processing fees," I said. "No wonder if they have to replace the bed every fucking time."

She giggled, moving weakly on the sticky mattress. She closed her legs and fumbled with the sheets until she finally freed one silky blanket and draped it over her body.

The fabric was so thin, I saw her pert nipples through it. My cock twitched, and I grinned. Not so spent after all.

"Um… I'll just go to the bathroom," Lucy said, her face growing bright red. I nodded, watching the color of her skin with interest that refused to wane.

Ice giants blushed blue. Her otherness was increasingly alluring, and I already knew I wouldn't tire from looking at her.

"Go on. We'll be on our way when you're ready," I said, giving her a nod.

She bit her lip, casting her eyes down, and quickly got up, wrapping the sheet fully around herself in a quick, efficient move. I caught a glimpse of her bottom and one slender hip, and she was gone.

"I need to get myself a human wife," Luca said once I put on my trousers. "I thought you would break her, but she took it like a champ. Really, I have to get one of those."

Sveg grinned and raised his arm. We bumped knuckles in a congratulatory gesture, and he clapped me on the back.

"Good job, brother. You'll finally get some fun after toiling all those years, aye?"

Ullag snorted at this, but I ignored him. He thought ruling the country was all nice dinners, expensive spirits, and females falling over each other to serve me. Even living by my side and watching how exhausted I was every day didn't disillusion him.

"Fun? Bedding a human female is a ton of trouble,"

I replied with a laugh, my mood too good to mind Ullag. "My legs will hurt tomorrow from doing my best not to crush her."

Luca, who was reading a pamphlet the priestess gave him earlier, put it away with a grimace.

"Not so eager to marry now, are you brother?" I asked with a grin.

"I'll think about it," he said. "If you're still happy a year from now, I'll apply."

The door to the bathroom clicked, and Lucy stepped out. She had a dress on, tailored similarly to the one I tore, but this one was red. The color made her blush seem hotter, and I just watched her for a moment, lost for words.

She was so different. And it only made me want her more.

"Come," I said, extending my arm.

She stepped hesitantly over, her lips pressed together. She stopped by my side and looked up, not taking my hand.

So tiny. I grinned, remembering how well my cock fit in that unassuming body.

She didn't take my hand, so I reached down and took hers, cradling it gingerly in mine.

"Go ahead," I said to my brothers, motioning at the door. "Maybe they have more pamphlets for you, Luca. Ask around. We'll catch up."

They left, and finally, it was just us: my human bride and me.

I looked down at her, and it didn't seem right to talk from such a distance, so I crouched, which made us almost equal. She took a shaky breath but didn't shy away now. Her eyes were boldly trained on my face, though her hand trembled in mine.

"Have you ever traveled through a portal?" I asked.

"It's how I got here," she answered. "From the temple in my city to the one here. Are we…?"

She didn't finish, but I understood the implied question. Usually, the bride traveled to the temple closest to where her husband lived. As portals were scarce, usually the couple would then go by train or car to the husband's abode.

"We'll go by portal," I said. "There is no temple in our lands. But there is a portal. It's right by the palace, so we won't have to travel far from there. How are you feeling?"

She stared at me, lips moving silently. It took her a moment to realize I asked her a question, and she blushed.

"I'm sorry," she said, casting down her eyes. "I mean, I heard who you are, I even spoke it, but… Palace? With its own portal? I'm afraid I will need some time to wrap my head around it."

Her blush was so very red, so warm, I could not resist. I leaned in and pressed my lips to her cheek.

We both gasped, I from the heat—she from the cold.

"We will both need some time to get used to this," I spoke against her skin, her shaky breath hot against my cheek. "But I want you to know… You are safe with me. I'll take care of you."

"Oh," she breathed so quietly, I wouldn't have heard it had my face not been pressed against hers. "Thank you."

"No need to thank me," I said with a smile. "It's only what I vowed to do."

"Well, I'll also keep my word," she said, her skin growing hotter.

My smile widened. She was so shy, she didn't even name her duties out loud, even though we just fucked in front of witnesses. Oh, how I hoped she would not stop blushing any time soon. It was my new obsession.

"On that note," I said, running my lips to her temple, "let's see about getting a big supply of that oil."

She giggled nervously, and I put my hand on her back and ran it down to her bottom, splaying my fingers wider over it. She gasped when I kneaded her skin, and I pressed another kiss into her.

"What do you think?" I asked, trying not to laugh as she shivered against me. "Should we?"

"Um… Oh!" she exclaimed when I squeezed her buttock, my fingers seeking the crease between her legs and running down it through the dress. "Yes, um, please. Oh merciful gods. What are you…"

"I'm just teasing you," I murmured, nipping at her perfectly shaped earlobe. "You're fun, little snowflake."

Lucy made a sharp sound and extricated herself from my hold. I grinned and then laughed, realizing she was affronted.

"Fun? Well, let me tell you one thing that's not *fun*. My legs are so weak, I can barely stand, and if you keep this up, I won't be able to *walk*!" She gave something between a sob and a laugh, and then groaned. "And it's all so *much*, and I didn't even wash properly, because there was just a small sink in the bathroom, and I wish…"

"I apologize," I cut her off, dropping my smile. "You've been through a lot. No more teasing for now —it's a king's promise. We'll go home immediately so you can rest. And bathe."

I couldn't hold back a grin at that, because the thought of her still being marked with my scent was too good, even if it made her uncomfortable.

Then I picked my little snowflake up. After all, she was as light as a mountain tiger kitten, and it was my fault she couldn't walk.

And everyone in the temple would know this.

CHAPTER 6

Lucy

I didn't protest when he carried me. My whole body was weak, and I was dizzy, head spinning. I had these dizzy spells sometimes, and when I saw the nurse in our village about that, she told me the same thing she told everyone: to eat more.

The problem with my health would probably be solved now, just like all the others. I settled into Aldrig's arms, and even though he was cold and not very soft, I felt like I could rest.

I still didn't know him. He was not just a stranger, but an alien to me. Even as he carried me through the torch-lit corridor, I was keenly aware of how tall he was as the ground swung far below me, making me queasy.

But I could already tell a tentative trust was building between us. He was gentle with me and made an effort to notice my needs. The way he treated me and spoke, even though we'd only exchanged a few words, made him feel less of a stranger. The easy camaraderie he had with the other giants felt familiar, too.

And yet... I sighed, discomfort squeezing my chest.

King. Why on Terra would an actual king get a bride through the temple? There had to be something wrong with him if he couldn't find a willing female among his own kind. It was the logical explanation.

I watched and listened as he bought the oil, spending over five hundred credits to ensure regular deliveries to his palace. I had to blink fast when the coins fell into a bowl with a clang, because I had never seen so much money in one place.

And he spent it completely without hesitation so that having sex with him would be painless for me.

Either he was *that* rich, or my comfort was important to him. Or maybe he was just practical. If he ripped me in half, I wouldn't be his wife for long.

We approached the portal, Aldrig's giants following us. There were more people here, humans and other races, but none as tall as my... well, husband. I would have to get used to the word.

They made way for us as we passed, most of them ogling Aldrig. When I heard whispers and giggles, I hid my face against his chest, the cold easing my blush.

I felt like such a fool. Wearing a pretty dress,

being carried around… That was not me. It was embarrassing.

And yet, a part of me enjoyed it. Somewhere deep, I thought that maybe, just maybe, I could rest now. Give some of the responsibility away.

Finally, we approached the portal. More money changed hands, and we were quietly led to the front of a short queue.

"Privileged travelers," said the portal pilot in a bored tone when someone in the queue grumbled.

He needn't have spoken. As soon as the humans saw Aldrig, they stopped their disgruntled mumbling and stared at their feet, avoiding his eyes.

"Everything is set, Your Majesty. You can go through."

"Let's go," Aldrig said, his voice cold.

I only had a moment to admire the portal—a beautiful golden arch, with gold and blue energy swirling inside—when we stepped through, and I was blinded by the light.

A few seconds later, we stepped out on the other side, and I blinked a few times, getting used to normal daylight.

It was still bright here. Fresh snow lay around the portal, making everything look pure.

And cold. I shivered, and Aldrig took off without a word, leaving the other giants behind. They called out farewells amidst laughter and lewd comments, but he didn't even look back.

The portal was in a small courtyard, surrounded from three sides by walls roughly the size of a giant, with a tall tower built of stone and black reflective material on the other side. We headed there, and when we reached the tower, a set of silvery doors opened, revealing a giant waiting on the other side.

He bowed, making me think he was a servant. We followed him up a staircase and then through tall, stone corridors with wide, glass windows, while the servant rattled off a list of information with numerous names and words I didn't understand.

It sounded like an update on everything that happened while Aldrig was away.

"And there is a fire burning in your chamber, as instructed," the servant finished.

"Thank you," Aldrig said in a cool, detached voice. "I'll deal with the Garags first. Tell them to come into the office."

The servant bowed and walked away, his steps echoing. Aldrig didn't say another word, and I gripped my dress in my hands, worried.

Was he angry with me for some reason? Or was he preoccupied with all the tasks the servant reminded him of? What was going on?

We reached a set of doors made of a white, shimmering material, and Aldrig opened them and stepped inside. He gently put me on the floor, bending low, and steadied me briefly with a cold hand over my lower back.

"I need to take care of some things," he said, not looking at me. "I will let you get settled. A human maid will be with you shortly."

And with that, he walked out, leaving me confused and angry. Was this how a husband treated his new wife?

I sighed and closed my eyes. We were married in name only, and he was clearly the more powerful part in our relationship. While the marriage was lawful, it didn't mean much apart from the fact that I would now live with him. And let him bed me whenever he wanted.

Gods, but I hoped it would be soon.

I opened my eyes with a shaky laugh and looked around, pushing my moping thoughts away. The room was mildly warm, not cozy by any means, but warmer than winter nights back home. There was a merry fire burning in a white marble fireplace, with a backup of wood arranged in silver wire baskets on the side.

I realized the fire was for me. Giants didn't need it as far as I could tell.

Forgetting my cold husband, I set out to explore. The room was spacious and bright, with a big, stylish bed right next to a vast window. I looked out and held my breath in awe.

The landscape was breathtaking. Ragged, snowy mountains loomed in the distance, their slopes gray stone covered with snow. Here and there, trees grew, dots of dark green against the white.

The sky was strange. It was still day, but it looked like the sun had already set, and beautiful, green and azure lights shimmered in the twilight.

I looked down. The bedroom was high, at least a few stories up, and below, I saw a big stone yard with giants standing and walking around. Some carried things, hurrying ahead, while others stood in groups, talking.

A flash of movement caught my eye. A child with bright blue skin ran, laughing, while a big male chased it with a grin. The child ducked between someone's legs, jumping over a big wheelbarrow that someone just rolled in, and kept running, until the giant finally caught it.

He spun the kid around in his outstretched arms, laughing, while it giggled. Then, he kissed the top of its head and walked off with the child in his arms.

I looked more closely, frowning. There were only males here as far as I could tell. Or maybe giant women just looked similar to the males, and I couldn't tell them apart?

The child seemed like a girl, though, now that I thought about it. It had hair—unlike the males I had seen until now. The hair was silver and wispy, and it looked kind of girly... But then, maybe all children had hair?

There was so much I didn't know.

There was a knock on the door, and a tall woman with bronze skin and kind eyes walked in. She wore a pair of black pants, a black sweater, and a white handkerchief at her neck.

She curtseyed with a smile, and I stared, unsure how to respond. No one *ever* curtseyed for me before.

"Hello, Queen Lucy," she said, looking at me with confidence. "My name is Abigail. I am your, well, maid is the official title... But I would prefer to think of myself as your personal assistant."

"Nice to meet you," I said after a moment of silence, during which I racked my brain for an appropriate answer. "Sorry, I just arrived and everything just happened so fast."

"Well, you're in one piece, which makes me very glad," Abigail said, looking me up and down curiously. "I know *some* giants that will lose a lot of coin thanks to this."

When I only blinked, she laughed and shook her head.

"I probably shouldn't tell you anything like that, to spare your sensibilities. But the way I see it, I am going to be your eyes, ears, and occasionally your fist, too."

"That's good," I said, still not getting her meaning.

"What I meant to say is that you are the first human ever to be married to an ice giant. And the king, no less. There were a lot of bets around the capitol, and let me tell you, most people expected you not to live through the wedding."

My cheeks felt hot, but I couldn't help but grin. Abigail was exactly what I needed to cut through all my bewilderment and help me find my footing. I didn't usually act like a lost lamb, and my survival skills were top notch, seeing as I lived long enough to be in my twenties.

But being in unfamiliar surroundings and situations took a lot of my confidence away. It was time to fix that.

"You're getting paid, right?" I asked, because that seemed important.

"Don't worry your pretty little head about it," Abigail said. "Your husband is loaded, and I am well-compensated."

"All right," I said, feeling more at ease. "So... I think I need a bath. And clothes. And you need to tell me everything you know about ice giants and these lands. Oh, and some food would be nice."

Abigail laughed, throwing her head back. I crossed my arms on my chest, wondering if I miscalculated and she wasn't actually here to do what I wanted.

"I'm sorry," she said after she finally stopped

laughing. "I'm just glad you're not one of those brides that have to be taught how to give me orders. I heard so many horror tales like this, you can't even imagine."

I shrugged, but secretly, I glowed with pride.

"Sorry if I came on too strong. I have five younger siblings, my parents are dead, and I'm the oldest. I know how to tell people what to do and expect them to act fast."

"No worries," Abigail said. "It makes everything easier. All right then! I'll show you the bathroom and I can tell you everything while you soak."

CHAPTER 7

Lucy

There was a hot water installation in the palace, Abigail informed me, that was originally put in to accommodate diplomatic guests. Before Aldrig applied for a human bride, he had warm water installed in his bathroom.

I soaked in the fragrant bath, relishing the heat and simple luxury. My home in the village didn't have plumbing, and I used to wash in a basin quarter-full of tepid water.

"The giants are just cold," Abigail said, arranging a pile of clothes on a chair by the enormous bathtub. "They say it's magic, but I know some scientists in the temples already studied them to find out how it actually works."

"And when they get angry, they get colder?" I asked, sliding down so that the water reached up to my lower lip.

"I suppose. I haven't touched an angry ice giant, so I'll have to trust you on that. I only know what I read. They brought me here two weeks ago."

"And why do you think Aldrig decided to get, well, me?" I asked, moving my limbs slowly through the water. I wanted to splash some around like a kid, but that didn't seem dignified.

"Oh, I can help with that!" Abigail said, her voice growing excited. "There were so many rumors, you have no idea! I didn't even have to ask around. I would just sit somewhere and pretend to read a book, and the servants would talk as if I wasn't even there… Anyway. Do you know how giants actually reproduce?"

I frowned at that.

"I assume a male giant puts his penis in a female giant's…"

"Yes, but apart from that!" she interrupted impatiently. "Oh, I can't believe you don't know. It's like the best system ever, and I am so envious! Right. So they reproduce like humans do, that's correct. But the thing with giants is that…"

She broke off, and I turned to shoot her an angry look. I already gathered Abigail liked to be dramatic, and her smile confirmed she withheld information on purpose now.

"Eat a bite of the meat and some beetroot, and I'll tell you. You have to eat if you want to get pregnant, you know," she said, a smile still playing on her lips.

I reached to a tray laden with food that stood on a small table by the bathtub. There were thin slices of cooked meat, small pieces of goat cheese, sugar-coated cranberries, and caramelized beetroot cut so thin, it was almost translucent.

I took a slice of meat, wrapping it around some beetroot, and stuffed it all in my mouth.

"Mhmg!" I signaled for Abigail to talk.

"So, they have very few females. It's just the way it is. For some reason, there are many more boys born than girls. The statistics say it's like fifty males to one female, so pretty dramatic rates. They've built their society around it. All the rules regarding mating, forming relationships, raising children… everything is built around this."

I swallowed and picked up another piece of meat to keep her talking.

"So what exactly does it mean? I don't follow."

Abigail grinned, practically glowing with self-satisfaction. I could tell she loved being the one who enlightened me. It was kind of cute. And only a little annoying.

"No monogamy. A giantess is like this godly creature that every male wants. So what they do is, they woo the females. They give them gifts, and jump through crazy hoops just to get one to sleep with them. Ice giant females don't have to work. They don't need money, because they get everything for free. Those giants worship the snow they walk on, I can tell you that."

I frowned, not quite comprehending how I fit in that system. Surely, a king would find no shortage of females to be with, even if they were so few and far between…

"So that's why I didn't see any females through the window," I said.

Abigail nodded eagerly.

"They are really rare. And the treatment they get, well, it goes to their heads. Your average giantess will get bored easily. They often travel from town to town, sampling from the goods all over the land, if you get my meaning."

I nodded, trying to put it all together.

"So… they don't settle for life?"

"No!" Abigail exclaimed with a laugh. "They don't have to! Gods, I am so green with envy… Anyway. How they get children: when a giantess finds a male with whom she wants to stay, or if she gets pregnant by accident, she will live with the father of the child until labor. Then she gives birth, stays a bit to breastfeed usually, and then she goes away. And the father raises the child."

I shook my head, the slice of meat I picked up earlier still in my hand.

"So the children… they grow up motherless?"

"Oh, I'm sure they don't mind," Abigail said dismissively. "Don't pity them as if they were human. This is a completely different race, Lucy. They have different needs. For example, children don't need a mother's warmth. They rarely hug here, you know. And if they do, it's usually a ceremonial gesture. Not one of affection."

I stuffed the meat in my mouth and chewed, but it felt flavorless in my mouth. No affection? Just what kind of nightmare did I get myself into?

"Anyway, as to why Aldrig applied for a match at the temple. It's all rumors, so it might not be true."

She lowered her voice and opened the door to look into the bedroom. She closed it and came closer, looking at me conspiratorially. I sat up, my curiosity growing.

"Aldrig's father was the king. He had him and another son from a different mother. Ullag. He lives in the palace, and I believe he was at the wedding."

I nodded, trying to remember if I heard that name. But it didn't matter, did it? If he was Aldrig's brother and lived here, I would see him soon.

"When a king dies, his son inherits the crown," Abigail continued, stealing one of my cranberries. "When there are more sons, they duel for the crown. Aldrig won, and Ullag has been sore about it all this time. At least, according to rumors."

She popped the cranberry in her mouth and chewed.

"People say Ullag has been a menace to Aldrig since then. He likes to rally the nobles against new laws that Aldrig wants to introduce, causing a lot of headache and unnecessary delay. Aldrig is a good king, or at least, that's what people in the palace say. He works hard and really tries to build a just, modern system that will benefit all. Ullag is more into oligarchy. He hangs out with the rich a lot.

"But back to you. So Aldrig had a girlfriend when his father died and he became the king. She was with him for a few months, and then Ullag lured her away in a very public way, which was humiliating for Aldrig. A year later, Aldrig had another girlfriend, and rumor has it, he wanted to marry her. See, kings can marry for life if they want. Days before the ceremony, Ullag did it again."

I lay back, frowning. Something didn't add up.

"But why a human wife, then?" I asked. "Does he expect me to be immune to Ullag's advances or what?"

Abigail took more food from the tray and chewed fast.

"Kind of," she said after swallowing loudly. "This is all conjecture, but from what I gathered, giants believe humans are naturally monogamous. See, it was easy for Ullag to seduce Aldrig's girlfriend, because she was used to hopping from male to male. And humans usually settle for life."

I finished my supper slowly while Abigail prattled

on about life in the castle, the food, and other trivial things. Even though I tried to listen, my mind kept going to what she told me about Aldrig.

I pitied him a bit, wondering how it must have felt to have a girlfriend—or fiancée, I wasn't sure about the right terminology— seduced so easily by his enemy. From what Abigail told me, I understood Aldrig couldn't even punish Ullag, because stealing away one's female wasn't really considered wrong. It was normal.

"But you're his wife now," Abigail told me at some point. "So if Ullag tries to seduce you, Aldrig can actually punish him. Different customs apply to wives."

I wondered if that was what Aldrig truly wanted. For me to give in to Ullag so he could finally punish his brother.

Or maybe he just wanted a faithful wife.

When I settled in bed, watching the play of brilliant purple and green lights against the night sky, I wondered what my life would look like. It was too early to tell, and the first day wasn't really indicative of much. But some things were already certain: I would not starve, and money wouldn't be a source of worry and sleepless nights anymore.

I was grateful for that.

It was chilly in the room despite the fire burning merrily, but the furs and blankets heaped on the bed were warm, so I snuggled under them with a sigh of relief.

Then I thought about my siblings. Was Daisy well? Did they already get the money? How were they dealing without me...?

And why was I alone in bed? This was my wedding night...

I slept through the night and woke up to Aldrig dressing quickly by the bed.

"Oh, you're here," I said sheepishly, tugging the blanket up to cover my chest. The pajamas Abigail found for me last night were quite revealing.

"Not for long," he said in a cool voice. "I won't sleep much until that blasted bill is done."

He looked up at me, and we looked into each other's eyes for a moment. Aldrig took a step closer, and a blush rose to my cheeks, because I thought I saw desire in his eyes.

He sighed heavily and stopped, simply looking at me. The cold in his face melted, shoulders loosening.

"How are you settling in?" he asked, picking up a set of wide, gold armbands that he tugged on his left arm.

"Everything is good, thank you," I said, eyes fixing on the gold band that slightly pressed into his biceps. For some reason, I found it extremely attractive, and knowing that piece of jewelry would have easily fit over my thigh made it even better.

"Abigail is wonderful, the food is amazing, and I slept like a log. Thank you," I said, putting all my emotion into it.

Because however distant he seemed, that one thing was certain. He took me out of poverty and helped my family. I would forever be grateful for that.

Aldrig nodded, a hint of a smile on his face, and turned away. He stopped, however, and turned back to me with a piercing look of assessment. Finally, he spoke.

"I've been working on passing a new land ownership law. There was some opposition, which made the matter quite difficult. I'm sorry if I'm absent over the next few days. Believe me when I say I'd like nothing more than to be here, getting to know you."

I nodded, a bit lost for words. It was sweet that he apologized. And I couldn't help but feel impatient for when he was finally done.

But some things were more important. I was the head of my family for long enough to sympathize. Responsibility was always more important than pleasure.

"Well, it's understandable," I said. "You have obligations. My mother always said: duty first, playtime later."

He grinned, ice-blue eyes sparkling in the morning light.

"I look forward to the playtime, then," he said. "In

the meantime, I need you to know I assigned a few trusted giants to you. They might stand outside this door or follow you."

"Why?" I asked, a bit alarmed. "Am I in danger?"

He gave me a tight smile and shook his head.

"Standard procedure. You don't have to worry."

Over the next few days, I saw glimpses of Aldrig in our bedroom. He mostly came in late at night and woke before me, and some nights, he didn't even come in to sleep. He updated me every few days in clipped words, briefly mentioning his grueling meetings with geologists, land assessors, economy experts, and lawyers.

He spent hours poring over documents, listening to those who had a stake in the bill, discussing matters with his advisors. Draft after draft was written, each rejected by one or more parties.

More estimations followed. More discussions. More drafting. And Aldrig was in the middle of it all, overseeing every aspect and directing the process so it wouldn't go astray.

Apparently, being a king of the ice giants on Alia Terra didn't mean you had absolute power.

He grew distant again, and we didn't talk much apart from quick conversations twice a week. Aldrig was clearly preoccupied.

Any soreness that was left from the wedding was long gone, and I explored my sexuality on my own during those long, lonely nights in my huge marital bed.

One day I realized I missed him, even though I barely knew him.

"Absence makes the heart go fonder and the pussy wetter," Abigail remarked sagely once I confided in her. "He knows what he's doing."

Abigail was very helpful. She wouldn't let me sit alone in my room, and I needed little convincing to go out and explore. We walked all over the palace, a silent guard always following us. We often visited the diplomatic wing, where I would sometimes see Aldrig rushing from one room to another or quarreling with another giant in the corridors.

Different rooms were taken by different experts, and Abigail informed me many guest rooms were occupied. The new bills were a big deal.

"He started working on it shortly before he got news they found his match. He dropped everything to get to the temple, but as things were already in motion, he had to keep going once you were back."

The new law was heavily opposed, Abigail told me. What Aldrig tried to do was end a feudal system in the country. About a dozen wealthy giants owned most of the land, and those who ran the mines in the mountains, mining for salt, graphite, and irrylium, a precious metal used for building portals, rented the land for exorbitant sums.

Aldrig wanted to change the law so those who actually ran the mines could buy the land. And those who only profited from owning the land and did nothing for the economy would slowly lose portions of their holdings.

"Ullag eggs them on," Abigail told me in a whisper when the infamous giant stormed past us one day, giving me a contemptuous look. "He just does it to piss off Aldrig, and to get money from those useless nobles, too. No one here likes him. He doesn't even deign to talk with normal people, only with those he deems on his level."

Apart from a formidable posture, Ullag also had a haughty air of superiority. He refused to look at other giants or the rare visitor of another race. His smiles were reserved for the nobles, and even I could tell they were fake.

After spending over three weeks in the palace, I was quite good at reading the giants. So it didn't surprise me at all that nobody liked Ullag.

Apart from roaming the palace and the gardens, we also ventured out to town. Once, we saw an ice giant female. Abigail pointed her out to me, an envious look on her face.

I immediately knew why she felt that way.

The female was slightly smaller than male giants, and she had long, white hair, braided skillfully around her head. She wore a pair of red trousers... and nothing else. Her large, well-rounded breasts hung freely, dark blue nipples hard.

But that was not what Abigail was jealous of. The female was surrounded by at least a dozen males, and they all gave her gifts, offering her a place to stay, inviting her to the theater or gladiator fights...

And she dismissed them all one by one, gathering the gifts she liked, leaving the others on the street, and walked away.

"Are they all like this?" I asked, staring after her with incredulity.

"Pretty much," Abigail said, shaking her head. "But it might change soon. More and more giants apply for human brides at the temple now that Aldrig did that. I expect that as soon as you have a baby, even more will try. But they need to see it's possible first. You know, they kind of look down on humans here. We are 'squishy' and 'warm-blooded'... But at least we don't trample on people's hearts."

We watched as one young giant picked up a beautiful, sparkling necklace from the ground, his face crestfallen. It was a gift discarded by the giantess.

Apart from sightseeing and gossiping with Abigail, I spent my days eating. Soon, I filled out enough for my assistant not to sigh with aggravation every time she saw me.

"Finally, you have some meat on you," she said once, pinching my hip. "Good. You can get pregnant now and cause a national rush for human girls."

She said it jokingly, but I didn't laugh. Over a month passed since the wedding. I didn't even see Aldrig anymore, and by now, I knew for certain I wasn't pregnant.

I filled my days as best I could. I wrote long letters to my family, telling them about the palace, the food, all the funny or exciting tidbits from palace life. I made sure to sound cheerful and happy in my letters.

They wrote back, telling me about their new life as livestock owners. Apparently, Daisy was growing fast now that she could eat eggs and drink milk daily. My brother did an excellent job taking care of everyone.

I missed them, but knowing they were doing well eased the burden.

When not writing letters or exploring, I tried to get busy making ice sculptures, which was an acceptable pastime for the queen. Though I was a queen in name only, and sculpting in ice wasn't my forte. At least, not the way the palace gardeners tried to teach me.

"This is the smallest chisel we have," the gardener said apologetically when I tried to lift the heavy tool, holding it in both hands. "I suppose we can have some human-sized chisels delivered, but it will take a week or two."

After that, my ice-sculpting turned purely theoretical. I watched as the gardeners showed me the proper techniques—and waited for the tools to arrive.

Once or twice, I thought I saw Ullag watching me, but he was as busy as Aldrig with the bill. They were in the final stages of preparing it. Aldrig was winning, and the law would pass soon, but he had to include some concessions for the nobles.

"It's not even their land," Abigail snorted one day when we saw a group of flustered giants talking animatedly to Ullag. "Their ancestors claimed it as theirs after the Shift. They have as much right to those lands as you or me. Well, less than you, actually. Since you're the queen."

I didn't feel like the queen at all. Because my only claim to the title was my marriage to Aldrig, and by now, the memory of our wedding seemed more like a dream than a real event.

Until one evening, Abigail ran into my bedroom with a shout of excitement.

"They passed it! The bill, it's official! Arag and Rourke are so happy, you can't even imagine. Their sons work in the mines, and they say this change will mean higher wages for them. Everyone's celebrating!"

I came over to the window. The courtyard was crowded with giants, and some of them were bringing out tables and beer barrels for an impromptu feast. Abigail bounced on her feet with joy.

"Come on, we should join them!"

I shook my head, feeling more like an impostor than ever. They were my people, and I was their queen… But I didn't deserve that title. I didn't deserve to share their joy, and going out there without my husband would feel incredibly humiliating.

Already, I knew giants whispered about me around the castle. A useless wife, I was called. Not attractive enough to hold her husband's attention. Not strong enough to bear his children.

In the light of Aldrig's absence, even though it was understandable, those whispers got to me.

But if Abigail was right, this would soon end. He would come back to me now. Just as he promised.

That thought made me perk up.

"You go," I said with a genuine smile. "Really, go out there. Be my eyes and ears. And I will… take a bath. Yeah."

Abigail didn't need to be told twice. And as soon as she was gone, I locked myself in the bathroom and got out a still unused bottle of the virgin oil Aldrig ordered from the temple.

Finally, I would have him back.

I quickly oiled myself up and dressed in a beautiful, lacy nightshirt. I unpinned my hair and let if fall down my shoulders. No longer thin and unattractive, it looked glossy and healthy now that I had access to food and cosmetics.

I looked at myself in the mirror, blushing already at the thought of Aldrig taking me like he did at the temple. My heart beating with excitement, I left the bathroom and stood by the window, waiting.

Soon, the door opened, and I turned with a smile. A muscular, blue giant stood in the doorway, looking at me with a grin.

I flinched and grabbed a blanket to cover myself, stumbling in my haste.

Because it wasn't my husband.

CHAPTER 8

Lucy

It was Ullag. For a moment, he just stood there, looking at me. Despite the wide grin on his face, his eyes were cold. They glinted with something cruel, and I took a step back, my instincts immediately recognizing the danger.
Shit.

My eyes darted around, looking for escape routes. He stood right in the doorway, so that was out. I was a few steps away from the bathroom, but even though I was closer to the door than him, his legs were longer.

If I dashed toward the bathroom, how fast would he follow me?

Too fast.

And if I locked myself inside, would he break down the door? It wasn't that sturdy. But it would probably take some effort, plus the noise might attract someone.

Noise. Should I scream? For a moment, I thought it seemed excessive. After all, he just stood there, and my instincts could be wrong.

Then again, he shouldn't even be here.

I glanced at the window, remembering the raucous party outside. The windows were soundproofed, and the doors muffled sounds pretty well, too. So if I were to scream, I had to do it now, while the door was still…

Ullag stepped inside and closed the door with a quiet click.

Shit, shit, shit.

"What are you doing here?" I said, trying to sound calm.

Because if we went straight to screaming and running, the game would be over before it truly began. It was in my interest to drag this out.

Ullag laughed, taking one step closer. I braced my shoulders to keep myself from flinching. If he kept talking, maybe it would give me enough time to… what, exactly?

Abigail was gone, having fun at the feast. She was the only one who came here—apart from Aldrig. How likely was he to come now? He promised me long ago that he would come as soon as the bill was dealt with… Or did he? Would he have to stay out there and celebrate?

And where was my guard? If Ullag was here, that meant he was missing.

Shit.

I clenched my jaw, glaring at Ullag, even though inside, I trembled. I had no delusions. If no one came to save me, I was doomed, because there was no way I could physically fight him off.

"My brother keeps taking things away from me," he said, his voice so sullen, it would have been pathetic if I wasn't so afraid. "So now I'm going to take something of his."

"I want you to leave," I said, standing so straight, my body vibrated with tension. "It's inappropriate for you to be here."

Ullag folded his massive blue arms on his chest and smirked.

"Make me."

I mimicked his posture, shoving my fear away.

Keep him talking. As long as he's talking, he won't do anything.

"You know that if you hurt me, it will give Aldrig an excuse to put you in your place once and for all? I'm his wife," I said, my voice sounding stronger than I thought possible in the circumstances.

But my legs shook. There was no hiding that.

"I want to see him try," Ullag said, his grin turning

into an ugly grimace while his face turned a darker shade of blue. "Because my fucking place is on that throne. And I have enough support to get it now. I just need him to do something stupid, which he will. He was always weak for the females. He will doom himself. And you will be the final snowflake, human girl."

I flinched. *Final snowflake.* The pet name Aldrig gave me sounded so foul in Ullag's mouth, but also—ominous. The final snowflake was a giant saying that meant something like the last straw.

If one snowflake too many fell on the slope of a mountain, it would start an avalanche.

That Aldrig himself gaveme this pet name seemed ironic now. If Ullag's plan worked, I would indeed be my husband's doom.

Before our marriage even started for good.

No. Not letting this happen.

I looked around again, taking in everything I missed in my previous sweep for escape routes. Surely, there was a way to fight him or slow him down. And if there was a way, I would find and use it.

Ullag laughed, taking another step closer.

"No can do, human girl. There's no way out of here. And no one's coming for you. My dear brother is basking in the glory of his victory right now. Raising toasts. Giving speeches. When he finally remembers his useless little wife, it will be too late."

He licked his lips, coming closer, and I stepped sideways, moving closer to the bathroom.

"You don't have to do this," I said, my voice breaking. I still didn't have a plan, and he was so close, and *oh gods*, his dick was hard. I saw the outline through his trousers.

"But I do," he said, prowling closer. I stepped aside, but he was so close now, I felt the cold emanating from him. It made me shiver. "Ever since he showed you off, I knew I would do this. And don't delude yourself. He knew exactly what he was doing, fucking you so I could see. He actually wants me to take you so he can get rid of me. But it won't play out the way he wants."

I felt sick, bile rising in my throat. Because Ullag's words struck a tight, painful chord inside me. I had this suspicion about Aldrig from the moment Abigail explained the relationship between him and his brother to me.

I dismissed it, then. But… he neglected me for so long. Was it truly his goal? To have Ullag defile me, so Aldrig could punish him?

Ullag laughed, his eyes gleaming with satisfaction.

"Not so stupid, aye, human girl? You're not so naïve as to expect he truly cares for you. We're alike, you and I. We can both see my brother for who he truly is."

He stopped. I was almost to the bathroom, and Ullag

was by the bed, one big step away from me. My heart pounded in my throat, my hands slippery with sweat.

"Tell you what," he said, assessing me. "Come to me willingly, and I will use that oil they gave him. I will make it feel good for you. Better than he ever could. And even better, you will live through it. What do you say?"

"Let me think about it," I said, dashing to the bathroom.

I threw the door open and was about to step inside when something yanked on the hem of my nightgown. I screamed, staggering back, and Ullag snarled behind me.

I gathered my strength and pushed toward the bathroom, tugging on my dress. There was the sound of ripping fabric, and I was propelled onward as the resistance vanished. I fell inside the bathroom and turned around, only to see Ullag charging at me, a piece of my nightgown crumpled in his huge fist.

No time to close the door. No time to think.

I grabbed the pitcher of oil that was still on the edge of the bathtub and threw it on the floor. The crystal burst into a million pieces, useless, because Ullag wore shoes, and anyway, his skin was too tough for the pieces to hurt him.

The oil spread in a shimmery, golden puddle on the floor.

Ullag bellowed and was through the door before I could even think of doing anything else. He stood in the puddle and wrapped his fist around my neck, lifting me effortlessly off the floor.

I kicked out, my throat squeezed shut. But even though I struggled with all my might, my legs didn't even reach far enough to scratch him.

Ullag's face filled my field of vision. Dark blue, hard, with manically burning eyes. He looked at me with hatred and panted.

"You could have chosen the easy way. Now… We'll see. Be good and I'll let you live through this. Defy me… And I'll fuck your corpse."

I kicked again, scratching at his stony fingers with my nails, but it was no use. I was already weakening, my head feeling ready to burst from the pressure, my body growing slack from the lack of oxygen.

Ullag grunted and reached for my neckline. With one sharp tug, he ripped the nightshirt off me, and through the oncoming darkness, I felt the cold gust of his breath on my chest.

There was a sound somewhere in the distance. An inquiring voice. Did I only imagine it? I blinked time and again, trying to keep the darkness at bay, and knowing it was useless, that I was going under…

Another sound. Far, far away, too far to reach me, and yet my heart tried to beat faster, to rouse me for one last fight because there was hope now. That voice... I knew that voice. It was Aldrig.

It had to be.

Ullag snarled and took a step forward. And then he gasped.

It happened so fast. One moment, he stood in the bathroom, and I was helpless in his grip.

A second later, we flew through the air, his grip on my neck weakening. It was a slow, dreamy fall, as if drifting through thick water. Suddenly, it sped up. I slammed into Ullag's chest, coughing, because I could breathe now.

He must have slipped in that oil I spilled.

I wanted to laugh, but couldn't. My throat was on fire, my lungs hurt, and I was too dizzy to think.

And I couldn't move yet, and so I had to stay like that, lying on top of the vile giant, but I could breathe, and any moment, I would get up and get help...

Someone grabbed me and hauled me off Ullag. I coughed again, gulping huge breaths when a pair of hard, cold arms enveloped me. I was completely naked, and I shivered violently from the cold, but it also helped me cut through the daze.

Suddenly, I saw the situation clearly, as if through the eyes of someone who had just come in. And who was that? I thought I heard Aldrig's voice, didn't I?

I shivered more violently, but not from the cold. Oh

no. If Aldrig saw us like this... Me, naked on top of Ullag...

Shit. Shit, shit, shit.

"What happened?" came the cold, angry voice of my husband.

CHAPTER 9

Lucy

"He attacked me," I said and immediately coughed again.

A cold, hard finger pushed my chin up. I gulped painfully and forced myself to meet Aldrig's gaze directly. I was innocent. No matter what his experiences with his former lovers and Ullag were, I did not cheat on him, and I would do whatever I could to prove it.

But in the pit of my stomach, I already had a sinking feeling of despair. He wouldn't believe me, would he?

When I looked into Aldrig's eyes, they were cold and alien. Closed off. He looked at me as if my mere presence disgusted him, and I clenched my teeth to keep myself from crying.

"He came here and said he would take me away from you," I said, the words urgent, even though my voice was horribly hoarse.

Aldrig looked away as a loud groan came from the bathroom.

"Put some clothes on," he said in the same alien voice, and then sat me down on the bed without looking at me.

I shivered again, suddenly wishing for a pile of furs to wrap myself in. He was so cold, his proximity burned, but now that he left my side, I felt even colder.

Aldrig went to Ullag. There was a loud thud followed by a groan. I realized I was just sitting there and staring, so I scrambled up, stumbling a bit before I found my footing, and quickly got to my wardrobe. I dressed fast despite the shaking of my hands.

Soon, Aldrig pulled an unconscious Ullag out of the bathroom. My mouth fell open when I saw a big, black welt on Ullag's cheek. It wasn't there before, and I quickly deduced Aldrig must have hit him.

Maybe not all hope was lost.

But then Aldrig looked at me over his shoulder with ice-cold eyes, and I shivered again.

"Follow me."

"Could we talk first?" I asked, panicking. I wasn't sure what he was up to, but judging by his anger, nothing good was coming.

"Later."

He turned and walked out, stooping slightly under the weight of Ullag.

I followed, trying to calm myself down. My throat hurt, and adrenaline still coursed through my bloodstream, making me jittery. Aldrig walked down the corridor and down the stairs, choosing the most direct route to the courtyard, and I gulped, walking fast to keep up.

If he said we would talk later, it had to mean he would listen. Right?

And yet... I stifled a whimper, because I knew what would happen. Aldrig had two lovers before me, and each of them were easily seduced by Ullag. It was only logical he would expect the same thing to happen with me.

Would he believe me if I explained what happened? And what if Ullag regained consciousness? He would spout lies, I just knew. He would tell Aldrig I gave in, just like those other females.

And then, I would be doomed.

I ran after my husband with my heart in my throat, cursing my stupidity. I should have never applied at the temple. *Perfect genetic match, my ass!* I should have tried harder, worked more, done something else to save my family!

Now, I was at the mercy of a husband whom I barely knew, because he was a king, and of course, the kingdom was more important than me.

Aldrig stepped out into the courtyard, dragging Ullag with him. I followed him through the door and stood back while the crowd of giants got quiet, all turning to watch their king.

He threw Ullag on the ground, and the giant groaned in pain, but didn't open his eyes.

"Today, my brother propositioned my wife," Aldrig said. He spoke in his normal voice, but it carried in the quiet. People stood motionless, listening intently. "I hereby banish him from the capitol and from the land, as is customary."

There were gasps and murmurs, and a commotion in the back. Some nobles pushed their way through the crowd.

"Luca, Sveg!" Aldrig said loudly. "Tie him up and take him away through the portal. He shall not gain entrance to the country as long as he lives."

"You have no right," said one noble, a small giant dressed in a red tunic. "There is no law against taking another's mate. You must have confused our lands with those of humans. Our customs are different, and a king should remember that!"

Aldrig laughed, shooting the noble a hard look. His laughter was so loud, it drowned out the whispers that broke out in the crowd.

"It seems I know our customs better than you do, Lord Rakr," he said mockingly. "For you seem to forget the position of a king's *wife* is treated differently. A wife only belongs to the king. If another giant lays his hand on her, he shall be banished. As our ancestral tradition dictates."

The noble gaped at Aldrig with an open mouth. Aldrig smirked, looking over his head at the watching crowd.

"If you need a quick revision course on our laws, you have my leave to reacquaint yourself with the proper scrolls. I'm sure we will be happy to wait for you."

"How do we know she is your wife?" another noble cried out, pointing an accusatory finger at me. "You married her in secret. For all we know, it could be a ruse to get rid of your rival. Everyone knows you hate Ullag."

"The marriage was witnessed. As was the consummation," Aldrig said, his voice gaining a sharp edge.

"I attest to the marriage," said Sveg, followed by Luca.

The noble in the red tunic must have recovered from his blunder, because he charged to the front, pointing his finger at Aldrig.

"Are you truly an ice giant?" he shouted, spit flying from his mouth. "You will choose a human female over a giant brother?" He turned to the crowd, spreading his arms wide. "What kind of king chooses a foreigner over his own kin? What kind of king will banish his brother on the word of a foreign wife? Maybe he should leave our lands and live among the humans!"

Before the murmurs in the crowd turned into cheers, as I suspected they would, Aldrig laughed again, his laughter reverberating in the courtyard.

Everyone got quiet.

"I accept your challenge, Lord Rakr," he said with a wide grin. "If you seek to run me out, we will duel. As is traditional, which I am sure you know well."

Rakr turned back slowly, his eyes wide. He looked at Aldrig, who stood straight, with his arms held loosely at his sides. Then he glanced at Ullag, who was still unconscious and held between Sveg and Luca, and finally, he shot a pleading look to the other nobles.

But they were all gone, dispersed in the crowd.

It was him against Aldrig. And Aldrig was bigger, meaner, and stronger.

"I forfeit," Rakr finally said, his face dark blue from humiliation.

"Wise decision," Aldrig said, growing serious. "Your first. Very well. As you forfeited our duel after challenging me, I strip you of your title and lands. Now get out of my sight."

When Rakr beat a hasty retreat, Aldrig nodded at Luca and Sveg. They lugged Ullag away, and Aldrig finally turned to me.

"Come here, Lucy."

I gulped, even more nervous than before. I watched the spectacle with bated breath, just like everyone else, almost forgetting I was in trouble, too.

On shaky legs, I approached him. Aldrig caught my hand in his, and an electrifying shiver went up my arm. For a moment, our eyes met, and he gave me half a smile.

What...?

"This is my wife!" he called out over the heads of other giants. "My human wife, whom I married before witnesses! She is my chosen, my beloved, the vessel for my heirs, and my future! Whoever lays a hand on her will be punished. If our union is challenged again, I will treat it as a challenge to a duel."

The courtyard was deadly quiet, and I was certain the giants standing in the front row heard the wild beating of my heart.

Aldrig squeezed my hand and tugged me closer.

"And now, if you will excuse me, I will take some time off. I have toiled over this bill for the last month and neglected the joys of mated life. My wife has been very understanding, for which I thank her, but neither she nor I have any patience left."

There were a few laughs in the crowd, and one encouraging shout. I blushed, and Aldrig chuckled quietly.

"If everything goes to plan, you can expect happy news soon," he said, which resulted in more laughter. "And now make merry and drink to my wife's health. She will need it!"

He led me back into the palace among cheers and applause, and my face was so hot, I was certain it steamed.

"Come, wife," Aldrig said, turning to me when we were inside, and the noise became just a distant buzzing. "We have much to make up for."

CHAPTER 10

Aldrig

When we got to the bedroom, she stood in the middle of the room, wringing her hands and looking anxious. Her blush was as delicious as it was that first time, and for a moment, my thoughts fled as my long-denied desire stirred to life.

But no. I had to make things right first.

I closed the door and walked over slowly. She looked up at me with a challenge in her eyes despite her emotional turmoil, and I smiled.

But then, I looked at the red marks on her throat, and my smile vanished.

"Are you hurt anywhere else?" I asked, tracing a finger across her throat, my touch gentle.

She sighed, taking my hand and pressing my finger into her reddened skin.

"Much better now when you cooled it. And no. You arrived just in time. I am good now. I feel safe," she said, raising her eyes to my face.

"What do you need?" I asked.

Even though I wanted nothing more than to spread my wife open and take from her everything I denied myself for a month, I would wait until she was ready.

She cast her eyes down and let go of my hand on her throat. I took it away and just watched as she swallowed tightly, clasping her hands together.

"Just... Stay with me?" she asked, looking up through her lashes. "Please."

I released a long breath, fanning the hair on her forehead. It was what I wanted, too, and it made me happy she chose my presence over loneliness or somebody else.

"You have me, snowflake. I won't leave your side."

She smiled, her eyes warming up. Yet, I couldn't help but still be angry whenever I saw the marks on her throat.

"He will not just be banished," I said evenly. "I couldn't prosecute him without causing an uproar. Which is why I didn't reveal he attacked you. That would require a trial, and I don't have patience for that. So Ullag will be dealt with quietly, in some faraway land where no one will demand vengeance for his death."

Her eyes widened, and she shook her head. I

frowned, unsure what that meant.

"Do you want me to spare him? Because I will not."

"It's not that," she said immediately. "I will be happy knowing I never have to see him again. And thank you. I just…" She dropped her eyes and stepped from foot to foot. Finally, she looked up, squaring her shoulders. "I'll just ask you directly. Please, be honest."

"I will."

"Did you do it on purpose?" she asked. "Were you counting on the fact he would attack me so you would have an excuse? I'm sorry to bring it up, because you believed me at once, and here I am doubting you, but I need to hear it from you."

I studied her for a moment, wondering how she came to that conclusion.

"Do you know how I knew you were telling the truth?" I asked instead. When she shook her head, I told her. "When I came here to finally be with you, I found your guard unconscious on the floor. I knew then that whoever entered our bedroom wasn't here at your invitation."

She rushed out a small breath, some tension leaving her shoulders.

"Is he all right?"

"The guard? He'll recover. And do you know why I had guards follow you everywhere and stand outside your door?"

"Because of Ullag?" she asked.

"Yes. I didn't know for certain he would try to hurt you. He never did such a thing before. But I didn't want to leave anything to chance. So no, I did not use you to get rid of my rival. I did not put you in danger, not consciously, at least, and I did what was in my power to protect you."

I took a deep breath, looking into her wide, vulnerable eyes.

"But I neglected you. You are my wife, and you were transplanted into a foreign land and burdened with the title of the queen. And I was in the middle of working through the bill. At the time, it seemed more important. I thought it would take a few days, not weeks."

She shook her head firmly, her hair bouncing.

"No, you were right to focus on that. Duty comes first."

I took her hand and bowed low to kiss her knuckles.

"I have a duty to my wife, first and foremost. I will not repeat the same mistake, Lucy. So please, forgive me"

She stroked my cheek with her fingers, her warm touch bringing long suppressed feelings close to the surface.

I longed for her warmth, craving her touch, and starved for her affection. And all that time, I denied myself because I knew: once I drank from the well of pleasure that was my wife, nothing would keep me away from her.

"Well, I was rather lonely," she conceded. Then, with a sly look, she added, "And horny."

I looked up, taking in her brilliant blush and wet, parted lips. Immediately, I knew the time for talking was over. My wife wanted me—just as I wanted her.

"See, Lucy," I said, straightening, so I could show her how hard I was. "I kept myself away from you with iron will. Because I knew as soon as I started fucking you, I wouldn't be able to stop. The kingdom could burn around us, and I would still not part with your hot little cunt."

She gasped when I pressed my cock into her breasts, growing instantly harder as soon as I felt the warmth of her body.

"Um, the oil," she said, breathing fast. "I shattered the bottle to make him slip in it."

I went to a cupboard where my supply was stashed. When I opened it, Lucy gasped, seeing the long row of bottles.

"Over a dozen," I said. "More is scheduled to arrive later." I turned to her, holding a bottle. "Because I will no longer deny my wife the pleasure she is due. I plan to bed you every day, more than once if you can take it. Because as the saying goes, absence makes the heart grow fonder. I've grown quite fond of you, wife."

Her blush grew in intensity, and she licked her lips, eyes traveling down to my straining cock. Then, without another word, she threw off her clothes and climbed on the bed. She got on all fours and arched her back, offering me a first class view of her lovely ass.

"So eager, little snowflake," I whispered, stalking closer.

"I waited for you," she said, her voice hoarse. "You might find I did a little preparing of my own."

As I leaned closer, I saw that, indeed, her red cunt already glistened with the oil. I palmed my cock in impatience, my vision growing dark for a moment. All I wanted was to plunge into her then and there.

But I made myself wait.

Slowly, I opened the bottle and poured some oil in my palm. I swirled a finger in it and pressed it into her opening. As my finger slid easily into her heat, my wife made a lovely, high-pitched sound. I gathered more oil and did it again. I prepared her for me, just as I did during our wedding ritual.

But she was more impatient now. She wriggled her hips and begged me with needy sounds, and soon, I worked her cunt with two fingers, thrusting them in and out to the sound of her moans.

Finally, I pulled them out and just looked at her. She was red and plumped, her opening stretched, yet still much too tight for my cock, I knew.

She would get used to it soon when I entered her. But for now, I had an idea how to help my wife relax even more.

"Wait a moment."

I bathed my cock in the oil and wrapped a towel around my hips. I brought her another one, and when she pulled it around herself, I took her hand and led her out of the bedroom.

The corridor was empty, and soon, we arrived at the hidden passage I hadn't used in a long time.

When I pressed the right panel in the wall and the passage opened, Lucy gasped with delight.

"I didn't know that was here, it's so well hidden," she said as I took her hand and led her inside. "Where are we going?"

"To a hot spring," I said.

We went down a few flights of narrow stairs and soon emerged on the snowy shore of my secret hot spring. Lucy shivered at once when the cold outside air bit at her skin. I picked her up, letting her wrap her legs around me, and impaled her on my cock until she grunted in protest.

I stopped, my length halfway in her heat. We both groaned, and for a moment, I swayed on my feet, overcome by the pure bliss of being enveloped by her.

The chattering of her teeth helped me regain my focus, though, and I waded in the water, submerging so that her entire body was under the surface, only her head out.

My snowflake hissed from the sudden change of temperature, and I took in a deep breath, letting the heat of the water penetrate into me.

White steam rose around us. Lucy stopped shaking and looked around in wonder. I leaned back against the closest rock and closed my eyes, enjoying the feel of her being pressed so close, of my cock being sheathed in her.

My lust thrummed under my skin like a pleasant current, and for a moment, I was perfectly content to just stay like that.

"It's incredible," Lucy said, shifting to put her legs more comfortably around me. My cock slid deeper inside her, and we both gasped from pleasure.

"The rocks hide it from view," I said, repositioning my forearm under her ass so she wouldn't slide further down until she was ready to take more. "And I thought it would be good for you. I know I'm cold and hard by human standards. I hope that at least here, you won't mind it as much."

"I don't mind it at all," she said, dropping a kiss on my chest as high as she could reach. "But this feels good, yes. Thank you."

She rested her head on my chest, and we stayed like that for a while. I enjoyed the softness of her against me, the hot water around us, and my cock, safely held in her sweet pussy, didn't show any signs of softening.

Soon, she wiggled her ass, and I let her slide lower. We waited like that until she moved again. Bit by bit, I pressed deeper into her until we were flush against each other.

I groaned, my lust growing sharper now, bringing me out of the luxurious stupor. Lucy reached down into the water and gasped as she felt the bulge through her belly. I felt the faint touch of her fingers as she traced my shape through her skin.

"You feel so good, snowflake," I murmured, lifting her higher. "I could stay inside you forever."

With that, I let her slide down my cock. We both moaned when her pussy devoured me whole, and I lifted her up again, hissing from the delightful friction.

I established a slow, even rhythm. The water slowed the pull of gravity, turning our hot spring mating into a torturous, exquisite experience that I wanted to last for a long time.

Soon, Lucy reached down again, and I watched her face as her blush grew, her lips parting, eyes glassy as she looked up. Her fingers on her clit, she brought herself to an orgasm, her cunt tightening around me so much, I had to bite my tongue not to come on the spot.

"I will flood this pussy with my cum," I told her

when she tightened and loosened around me in waves, panting from pleasure. "I will come so deep inside you, you won't have a choice but to take it all. You will have my children, snowflake. I will put them in this cute little belly of yours."

She threw her head back, nails digging into my forearms as she grabbed them. I moved faster now, clenching my jaw from the effort to make it last, but the vision of her being full of my cum, creamed so well it gushed out of her, brought me close to release.

I couldn't hold back.

"I will fuck you every day until you're pregnant, wife," I said through gritted teeth, fucking her as fast as our position allowed. "And then, I will fuck you every day to keep reminding you that you're mine. This pussy is mine. This womb is mine. This warm little body is all mine."

She let out a guttural moan and clamped tight around me, another orgasm gripping her.

I groaned, no longer able to hold myself back. I held her firmly and fucked up into her, shoving my cock as deep as it would go and releasing streams of cum into my wife's fertile body.

I pulled her closer, breathing hard as my balls tightened, the echoes of my orgasm filling me with languid heat. Lucy gave soft moans, still tight around me. I brought my hand down to caress her belly and froze in wonder.

Her shapely human belly was inflated, pushed outward. It wasn't just my cock filling her, it was something more. She felt as if pregnant already, and for a moment, my mind blanked out, uncomprehending.

And then I realized it was my cum. It filled her to the brim, and since my cock was still lodged deep inside her, with her pussy tight around it, my cum had no way out. It was all inside her, filling her close to bursting.

"Snowflake? Are you all right?" I asked, suddenly worried.

Human bodies were not made to hold so much volume, were they?

"Good," she mumbled, her head moving weakly against my chest. "The best. So full. I love it."

"You're not in pain?" I kept asking, my fingers gingerly tracing the curve of her belly. "Nothing inside feels wrong?"

"It couldn't feel more right," she sighed, nestling into me. "I'm so full… So content. For the first time, I feel complete. Let's stay like this."

I caressed her back and shoulders, and even though I came so copiously inside my wife, my cock remained hard and eager. The thought of my wife being full of my cum like this made me want to fuck her again and again.

Soon, she stirred. I pulled out of her, letting the

excess pour out of her, and then I fucked her again.

She was mine, and I would show it to her every day. My wife, my treasure.

My love.

LUCY'S EPILOGUE

I leaned over Daisy to make sure she was asleep. My youngest sister adjusted well to life in the palace, but even so, she couldn't fall asleep without me.

She suffered in my absence. But now, she was here, and I could take care of her as I had always done.

As soon as my siblings arrived through the portal, brought here in secret by Aldrig, Daisy launched herself at me and refused to let go for hours. She missed me terribly. And even though my other sisters did all they could to comfort her, she still couldn't get used to a life with me gone.

But now, they were all here. Aldrig noticed how I missed them, saw how often I wrote and received letters, and finally asked me casually if my brothers and sisters would be opposed to moving.

I told him nothing really held them in our home land. Our parents were dead and cremated, their ashes scattered. The house my siblings lived in didn't belong to them.

He dropped the subject. A week later, my brothers and sisters were here, moving into rooms in the palace that Aldrig designated for them.

I smiled, caressing the small curve of my belly. Quietly, I tiptoed out of the room and paddled to our bedroom, where Aldrig was already in bed, waiting for me.

"How are you feeling?" he asked at once.

Ever since I told him I was pregnant, he refused to leave my side for longer than a few minutes. We went for weekly check-ups in the temple, where biology experts who studied interracial reproduction monitored my pregnancy. For now, they said it developed perfectly with a very low risk.

And still, Aldrig couldn't be peeled away from me. He delegated as many tasks as he could, and when he had to deal with something personally, he brought me with him.

Now, he called me to the bed, arranging the hot water bottles that were our way of dealing with the temperature difference. I slipped between the sheets, pressing my back into his front, pushing an electric blanket between us. We lay like that until Aldrig stirred impatiently.

I smirked. I felt his cock grow hard as soon as I lay down, and only waited for him to finally lose control.

"In the bedside table," I murmured.

He turned away, shuffled here and there, and a moment later, a cold finger slick with oil pressed into my core, making me clench with arousal.

"Tell me at once if you don't feel well or…" he started, but I pressed myself into him, making him groan as my body pushed into his cock.

"Stop worrying and fuck me. Please, my king," I said without a hint of reverence in my voice.

He growled and thrust his fingers deep, making me moan. Soon, I was ready, and he guided his cock into me.

We made slow, gentle love, and when Aldrig came inside me, he didn't pull out. I fell asleep with my husband's cock deep in my pussy, warming it so he could relax and let go of all his burdens.

And all was well.

ALDRIG'S EPILOGUE

I ran around with Evie sitting on my shoulders and laughing her three-year-old heart out. She held my ears in her little fists and directed me left and right, and I followed her cues to the point of gently walking into the wall when she directed me that way.

She squealed with excitement, and I laughed with her, making a sharp turn when she tugged my ear left.

Lucy sat on the bench nearby, breastfeeding little Caspian. He was asleep in her arms, and still, his soft blue lips refused to let go of her nipple, sucking even through his sleep. He was a big boy, growing seemingly every day. Lucy joked she had to eat for three to keep up with his appetite.

A shriek of joy drew my attention. It was Rijan, and

he carried Daisy in his arms as if she were a little babe. They were the same age, but he was twice as big as her, and he often used it to his advantage.

Daisy screamed for him to let go, but she laughed, so I decided not to intervene. Soon, she elbowed the unsuspecting Rijan so hard in the ribs, he lost his hold on her. As nimble as a snow cat, she slipped out of his arms and ran away, shrieking with laughter.

I smiled, giving Lucy a knowing look. She returned my smile with a wink.

Whatever Rijan's and Daisy's friendship would become as time passed, it was a welcome sign of the changing times. Our population grew rapidly, with more and more humans taking places in our society. Previously reserved and closed off, ice giants welcomed the newcomers. New families were started every day, with giants taking human wives.

And a new generation of unprejudiced youths was growing up. Giants and humans living side by side, working toward a better world.

I smiled at my wife and sent a quiet blessing her way.

And all was well.

KEEP READING

Wed to the Ice Giant is a book in the *Arranged Monster Mates* series brought to you by paranormal, fantasy, and science fiction romance authors. If you liked this world and tropes, explore the other books in the series for more steamy arranged marriage monster romance novellas.

THANK YOU FOR READING AND REVIEWING!

BOOKS IN THIS SERIES

Arranged Monster Mates
The Temple, a matchmaking service for monsters, shifters, and aliens, is open for service.

Arranged Monster Mates is a series of novellas written by your favorite paranormal and sci-fi romance authors: Eden Ember, Layla Fae, and Cara Wylde.

Each of these steamy stories has it all: a possessive male, a heroine ready to sacrifice herself to the beast, plenty of spice, and a happily ever after to curl your toes!

Wed To The Orc By Layla Fae

My tiny new wife is a force of chaos bent on turning my life upside down.

I am a researcher. I read books, conduct experiments, and live quietly on the fringes of the orc town. All I want is peace, quiet, and a female to satisfy the wild urges of my orc body so they don't distract me from my work.

Getting a human wife through the Temple seems like a logical solution—until I bring her home and she starts sowing chaos. She moves my books, cuts my herbs to make bouquets, and replaces the blessed silence with laughter and song.

For such a tiny person, she can be very loud. And opinionated.

Worst of all, she does nothing to calm my libido. Instead, she makes my body eager and my mind obsessed. She encroaches on my space, my work, my thoughts, and worst of all, my heart.

I hate being out of control, yet with her, it's all I can be. This cannot go on.

Something has to give.

Wed To The Lich By Layla Fae

Every living thing is repelled by my corpse-like body... but not my wife.

Liches are almost gone, only a handful of us left. I must marry to keep my race from extinction, yet how? No living female will ever stoop so low as to marry a lich. People fear us. They say we are the harbingers of death, bad luck, rot and decomposition.

In one last bid to carry out my duty, I request a wife through the Temple. She turns out to be a neglected, sickly thing with trembling hands and downcast eyes, seeking an arranged marriage out of despair.

And she's perfect. Her blushes burn hot, her voice rings with feeling, and her kisses taste like summer. She is life personified, all warmth, light, and sweetness, and I crave her like darkness craves the sun.

But will she sacrifice her warm, beating heart to a creature of death like me?

Wed To Jack Frost By Layla Fae

I just wanted to win a stupid bet – and now I have a wife?!

I made a drunken bet. The Yule was nigh, and Yule's the time when Frost men drink mulled wine and dare each other to stupid stunts. My brother bet I'd be too scared to send a blood sample to the Temple, so of course, I proved him wrong. And before I sobered up enough to withdraw my application…

Ping!

I got matched.

So now I have to go up there and explain to the hapless woman who's apparently my perfect mate that I'm in no hurry to get married. I'm only 54, goddammit! Who even marries so young?

Me, as it turns out. I do. Because the bride that fell in my lap like the most perfect Yule present won't let me leave. She's a harridan and one hell of a bossy shrew who pummels me with cute, lust-provoking

insults, and I...
I think I'm in love.

Wed To The Basilisk By Layla Fae

No one touches my bride. No one but me.

I am the last basilisk on Alia Terra. As I roam my lands, loneliness muddles my mind and pumps violence into my veins until I don't recognize myself. Soon I'll become a feral beast – unless I mate.
The matchmaking temple is the only way a creature like me, scaly, fanged, and with lethal eyes, can marry. Soon, I have a match. My temple bride is everything I dream of: sweet, resolute, her delicious scent calming my rage with the first inhale.
It seems like it will work out until a human male barges in the temple, grabs my bride so hard she cries out, and tries to drag her away. My fury burns too hot to control. I unleash my lethal sight, killing him on the spot.
My bride is terrified, cringing away from me. Will she ever trust me again after this?

Wed To The Minotaur By Eden Ember

I arrive on Alia Terra tempted by the promise of fertile land and females.

Filled with longing, I cannot rest until I find a sweet mate just for me. One who will warm my bed at night, one for whom I will build my fortune under the scorching sun.

There is only one way to meet a perfect match: the Temple. I do the test and focus on building a prosperous ranch for the female who is destined for me. She will have the best of everything.

The wait is long. Long enough to lose hope.

And then, the letter comes. My mate is ready to be claimed, and I set out immediately. Nothing can stop me now.

When I see her, my blood burns with desire, and the instinct to make her mine overshadows everything. She is precious, perfect, and too beautiful to be true. She is everything I could have dreamed of.

I will never let her go. I will pamper, love, and caress her until every inch of her body belongs to me. No other male will drink from her nectar. No other will plunge deep into her sweet depths.

I will claim what's mine.

Wed To The Wolfman By Cara Wylde

Alone.

Even surrounded by my devoted wolves, I feel alone and forsaken. The legends of my clan say that an Alpha without a mate will wither in time, and weakness will infect him until a stronger wolf will challenge and dethrone him.

I cannot allow that to happen.

I've searched for my mate far and wide, and when I

couldn't find her among my species, I turned to the walled cities of the humans. They are filled with fair, fertile females, but none of them smells or feels like my mate.

There is one last thing I can try. The Temple. Can a simple draw of blood match me to my fated mate? I don't believe it.

Until I see her. She is beautiful, fierce... She is untamable. Her scent tells me all I need to know.

She is mine.

BOOKS BY THIS AUTHOR

Draco: A Dragon Chef Romance

My boss is a dragon and he tastes like magic.

When I say I'm clumsy, I'm not being cute. With the amount of things I have tripped over, dropped on myself, and fallen into, it's a miracle I am still alive.
So how did I end up working in a restaurant kitchen? And not just any kitchen. It is run by the notorious chef Draco Domanski, who cannot abide people tripping on asparagus or spilling coffee down his shirt.
Draco can't stand my klutzy ways. Sowing chaos in his precious kitchen, I've come to know the signs of his monstrous displeasure. Eyes gleaming red. Smoke fuming from his nose. Tail wrapping around my leg while he growls threats in my ear, making delicious shivers run down my body.
But no matter how furious I make him, he won't let me go. Soon, I discover why he needs me. I learn his other mouthwatering secrets: that he is doubly

endowed and tastes like heaven.

Draco is passionate, tenacious, and… I can't fall for him. He is my boss, keeps calling me Rabbit, and his fangs could rip me in half.

If I ignore the tension cooking between us, it will go away. Right?

Guarded By The Snake: Monster Security Agency

She stole her way into my cold, serpent heart like a thief in the night.

The tiny human hires me to shield her from the vengeance of a powerful organization. There's nothing wrong with that, except she stole from them, got caught, and now I have to clean up her mess. Add to that her incessant chatter, and I'm in for the most unpleasant job in my career.

Until her enemies bring out the big guns, turning the irksome protection assignment into a lethal fight for survival. Necessity pushes my principal closer and closer—too close for comfort. Forced to hide in small spaces, her skin rubbing against my scales, her warm breath on my face, my exasperation gives way to lust.

It's just physical attraction, I tell myself. All I want is to bury my two spikes in her tight body and feel her writhing under me in pleasure. Nothing more than that. Because it's impossible I could want her–the annoying, ballsy little thief who makes the sun shine with a smile.

One thing is certain: this is no longer just a job. I'll butcher everyone who wants to hurt her.

Devil's Deal: A Dark Fantasy Romance

The devil craves my soul. It calls to him like the scent of fresh blood.

I am not afraid.

The night of summer solstice, I do something stupid. Drawn to the power and fire of magic, I dance with the gods. I am not important enough to merit their attention.

But someone else is dancing, too. His fiery eyes burn into me as black paws circle my waist, turning me to the beat of his hooves. For one night, and one night only, I let him touch me.

When it's morning and gods return to their shrines, he stays. His menacing shadow follows me, a dark cloak hiding me from the sun and the light of hope. Where I walk, flowers wither and children sicken, touched by his suffocating darkness.

The more I chase him away, the more he enshrouds me in his dark, powerful presence, whispering words of seduction in my ear.

He has something I badly need, but his price is too high. This deal might break me.

FREE ROMANCE NOVEL

I wrote a free djinn romance novel called *The Third Wish* that's free to download for everyone! Expect the following: paranormal romance, djinn / furry monster shifter MMC, bubbly sunshine FMC, high spice, knotting, suspense and action, initial enmity between the heroes, hurt and grovel by the MMC.

Premise: the FMC summons a djinn by accident. He hates being a slave so he threatens her, and to save her life, she makes a very dangerous wish that backfires delightfully, resulting in some very spicy scenes.

Download from my website www.laylafae.com. It's free!

www.ingramcontent.com/pod-product-compliance
Ingram Content Group UK Ltd.
Pitfield, Milton Keynes, MK11 3LW, UK
UKHW021433280725
7111UKWH00009B/77